WRAP-IT-U

LOST & FOUND

WRAP-IT-UP MAGIC

LOST & FOUND

Jane Glatt

TYCHE BOOKS LTD.

Lost & Found
Copyright © 2024 Jane Glatt

All rights reserved. No part of this book may be reproduced or transmitted in any form or by any means, electronic or mechanical, including photocopying, recording or by any information storage & retrieval system, without written permission from the copyright holder, except for the inclusion of brief quotations in a review.

The publisher does not have any control over and does not assume any responsibility for author or third-party websites or their content.

This is a work of fiction. All of the characters, organizations and events portrayed in this story are either the product of the author's imagination or are used fictitiously.

Any resemblance to persons living or dead would be really cool, but is purely coincidental.

Published by Tyche Books Ltd.
Calgary, Alberta, Canada
www.TycheBooks.com

Cover Art by Niken Anindita
Cover Design by Indigo Chick Designs
Editorial by M.L.D. Curelas

First Tyche Books Ltd Edition 2024
ISBN: 978-1-989407-76-9
Ebook ISBN: 978-1-989407-77-6

Author photograph: Eugene Choi Echo1 Photography

For everyone who has ever had to start over.

CHAPTER 1

HEAD BOWED AGAINST a cold late November wind, Barb dragged her suitcase down the driveway of what had been her home for twenty years: a lovingly kept Victorian mansion in Rosedale. A place where she'd hosted countless parties and charity events.

A house that was no longer hers.

The gate was open—the court appointed movers had arrived bright and early that morning—and five trucks were lined up in the long driveway.

It was a relief, in a way. It had been difficult and humiliating showing the appraisers around, ensuring that they had all of the documentation for the more expensive pieces of art and furniture. She'd always thought it was a good thing she'd been a meticulous recordkeeper since Richard had been terrible at it.

She snorted. Now she knew that her husband's haphazard recordkeeping was on purpose. It had taken forensic accountants months to untangle enough of his finances to finally charge him.

Embezzlement: a fancy word for stealing. It turned out that Richard had spent most of his life stealing: from investors, friends, neighbours, and at the end—when his Ponzi scheme was unravelling—from his own children, because of course even they weren't off-limits.

She was certain they hadn't found all his money: there was no way Richard would have fled the country without some sort of nest egg stashed away somewhere in the world. It wasn't as though he'd be willing to live off whatever his most recent girlfriend could make as a waitress.

That's how he usually met his unending string of paramours: during one of his numerous outings at bars and restaurants where he flashed money around, impressing susceptible young women.

She'd known about them for years and had resigned herself to his philandering mostly because she figured that she had always known who he was. It was her fault for marrying him, but she'd done so willingly in order to escape a less-than-happy home and an angry and controlling father.

Back then Richard had thoroughly charmed her and brought her into the centre of his circle. After her unhappy teen years, she'd enjoyed the lifestyle and attention that came with the society parties and extravagantly luxurious vacations. For most of her life she'd felt that the trade-off was worth it, but when she didn't, when the other women became too much to bear and she threatened to leave, Richard would once again turn the full force of his charm on her.

When he begged her to stay, when he promised to reform, she'd always believed that despite straying so often, he truly loved and valued her.

Now she knew it was because a divorce—and the need to disclose assets—would have exposed his larceny.

She was so stupid.

That was how she'd felt through the last excruciatingly painful six months. *Stupid.*

How could she have not known what her husband was up to? How could she have had no clue that he'd created a financial house of cards that had taken so much from everyone in Richard's orbit, including her?

No one believed she'd been that stupid: not her society friends; not the courts; not even her sons. Richard Jr. and Kyle blamed her for not warning them about their father; for allowing him to steal thousands of dollars from them. Now they wouldn't even take her calls so she could explain. Not that she knew what to say. How could she make them understand that there were so many things she'd just let Richard handle? How to convince them that she hadn't even known the house had been remortgaged and that her name had been taken off the deed?

That had been the final blow. She'd been evicted from her own house; a humiliation she wasn't sure she would ever recover from. The only silver lining was that she wasn't on the mortgage.

Richard had stolen everything from her: her home, her life, her friends, and even her family.

A car honked from the end of the drive and Barb waved. There was one thing, one person Richard hadn't stolen from her, although she was ashamed that she'd let him come so close.

Kat Henderson had been her best friend all through school. After Barb married Richard, she and Kat had drifted apart and hadn't reconnected until meeting up at their high school reunion half a dozen years ago.

That was when Barb learned that Richard had told Kat to stay away: that he'd deliberately sabotaged their friendship. Worried that he'd try to do the same thing again, she'd kept their rekindled friendship a secret.

Barb took one last look at the house she'd been so proud of, before stepping past the open gate to the waiting car.

"Ready to start your new Dickless life?" Kat asked from the driver's seat.

"I have to be," Barb said. She opened the back door, tossed her suitcase onto the seat, and got in the front.

"It'll be fun," Kat said. "You'll see."

"Fun," Barb repeated under her breath as she buckled the seat belt. She'd appreciate stable. She had very little money, no paid work experience, and a single friend who had stepped up far beyond anything she had any right to expect. She was sixty-two years old, and instead of looking forward to enjoying her golden years, she was staring directly at poverty. She didn't expect fun to be part of her life for a very long time.

Just three days later, Barb parked her new-to-her car in the driveway of Kat's yellow brick bungalow, a place she was not quite ready to call home even though she expected to be living here for the foreseeable future.

The Niagara Escarpment rose up behind the house, the so-called *mountain* in Hamilton. It had been Kat's childhood home, inherited after her mother passed away, and a place that Barb had fond memories of.

Barb got out and joined Mitch, Kat's daughter, who stood in the drive staring at the six-year-old, red, Nissan Versa hatchback.

It was a lot flashier than any car she'd ever had before. Richard had always leased elegant high-end BMWs for her.

The court had allowed Barb to keep one car, and she'd selected Richard's five-year-old Mercedes. He'd owned it outright so she'd had her lawyer sell it. The close to thirty grand she'd gotten for it would not last long, especially now that she'd bought another car, but at least for now, she could pay her own way.

"Is your insurance all squared away?" Mitch asked.

"Yes, thanks so much for your help." Buying cars was one of far too many things Barb had let Richard handle. Mitch had not only helped her buy the car and driven her to pick it up, but she'd walked her through all the paperwork. Now all Barb had to do was get it registered in her name. "I can't believe you got it for me for less than eight thousand dollars." She'd been expecting to pay over ten grand for a car, so this was an unexpected bonus.

"It was a good price because not too many people want standard transmission these days," Mitch said. "Lucky you know how to drive a stick shift."

"Lucky, sure," Barb replied. "It's nice to know that those European vacations were good for something. Twenty years ago, it was almost impossible to rent an automatic overseas." She shrugged. "And Richard liked to show off by having me drive his friend's high-end sports cars. Maserati owners are transmission snobs."

"It's here!" Kat called from the open door. "You should have called me. It's very cute."

"I prefer the word sporty," Barb said. She grinned. "I'm starting to feel like a grown-up." She even had high hopes to eventually be self-sustaining. Kat had talked her into wrapping gifts at the Christmas Fair that started this Friday. "Better late than never."

Barb had done plenty of gift-wrapping for charities over the years, and Kat, who was a long-term vendor at this fair, swore that it was something she could charge money for.

"Being a grown-up isn't what it's cracked up to be," Mitch said. "When you're young, you think it's about staying up late and sleeping in. The reality is it's all about making enough money to pay your bills so you can get up the next day to make enough money to keep paying your bills."

"Finally!" Kat exclaimed. "My daughter understands. My work is done."

"Then you read the wrong parenting books," Mitch replied. "Your work as a parent is never done. Right, Barb?"

"Right," Barb replied, but the joy had gone out of the moment. She would love to be parenting her own grown children but they wouldn't even take her calls. Neither one of them had even acknowledged her email with her change of address. She checked her watch: it was just after two. "I have things to do if I'm going to be ready for Friday. Unless anyone wants to tag along, I'm going to head out in my new-to-me car and get some of it done."

"Good luck," Kat said. "Mitch, can you stay for coffee or tea?"

Barb waved as she pulled out of the drive.

It took her all afternoon but when she pulled back into the driveway, she'd completed the car ownership transfer as well as her change of address for her driver's license and health card.

She also had a large bundle of wrapping paper, ribbons, bows, and gift tags along with various coloured tapes and markers for her new business as a professional gift-wrapper.

She was starting to get excited about it, which surprised her. She'd assumed that it would take years for her to experience even small joys, and here she was, just three days after being forced from her home, smiling and humming along with Christmas carols on the radio. All because she was trying her hand at a business. She was starting in a very small way but it gave her so much hope for the future.

And it was all due to Kat.

"Kat," Barb called when she shouldered the front door open, "are you home?"

"In the studio," came the muffled reply.

Barb left her purse and purchases on the kitchen island and followed Kat's voice to a door just past the kitchen. She opened the door and stepped down into what at one time had been a single-car garage. Now a work table stretched along the far wall and various tools hung from hooks above it. A tall shelf unit contained cubby holes filled with tiny plastic drawers.

Kat sat hunched over the table, a bright light shining on whatever she was working on.

"Be right with you," she said.

Barb wandered around, investigating rolls of wire and small bins of coloured beads and costume gems.

"Done," Kat said and sat up. She pulled off a pair of gloves and sighed. "I'm trying to make sure I have enough merchandise for the Christmas season. I always seem to leave it to the last minute. Did you find what you needed?"

"There was a store downtown that had exactly what I was looking for," Barb said. "And all of it without the Toronto prices." She spied a sign that read *Kat's Custom Jewelry*. "Oh no, do I need a sign?"

"That's actually a good idea," Kat said. "I have some letter stencils around here somewhere and there's plenty of craft paper."

"I better make a sign," Barb said. "I guess I need a name. And maybe an actual registered business."

"Eventually, yes," Kat said. "But if you want, you can just have your sales for this weekend go through my business and we can sort it out later. I can just add you as a supplier."

"Thanks. I'll think about it." She didn't want to cause more work for her friend, but there were so many new things in her life that she wasn't surprised she hadn't thought everything through. "By the way, I want to offer complimentary gift-wrapping to all of your customers. It might give you an edge over any competitors."

"Hey, I appreciate that but you don't have to."

"It will help me too," Barb said. "One, I won't be sitting around for two and a half days, and two, it will give me a chance to show what I can do. Three, it will be a small way for me to start repaying you for everything."

"You know I don't expect you to repay me."

"I know," Barb said. "But *I* do."

CHAPTER 2

THE NEXT TWO days went by in a blur. Barb decided it would be better to start off as a business, so she registered it and opened a bank account. The name she chose—Wrap-It-Up Magic—was a nod to how her work had been described for charity events: magical, enchanting, charming.

She made herself a sign and because she used some of her nicest wrapping paper on it, at the last minute she decided to venture out to buy more. She didn't even have time to take it out of her new car before she was due at the Christmas Fair. She parked in the vendor delivery zone and headed inside the old warehouse to look for Kat.

"Wow," Barb said. "Your booth is front and centre."

"I've been coming here for years," Kat said. "And I have a following." She shrugged. "Plus, I pay extra for the spot."

"Now you have to let me reimburse you for this." The list of how Kat was helping her was growing longer every day. Barb had no idea how she was ever going to repay her friend.

"I booked this booth last year," Kat said. "So it has nothing to do with you. How much space do you need?"

"I need a table at the back to work on and spot to hang my sign," Barb said. "When I'm set up, I'll wrap up a couple of your boxes as samples. Earrings and a necklace maybe, and you can just place them where you think it makes sense."

"I'll go arrange a table for you," Kat said, "while you bring your supplies in."

"Okay." Barb headed back out to her car. It took her two trips to bring everything in. Kat was nowhere to be seen, so she propped her bags and rolls of paper against the front table and went to find her car a more permanent parking spot. When she returned, Kat was directing two young men on where to set up a folding table.

"That's perfect," Barb said. She stepped closer to Kat. "Did it cost extra?"

"No. Three tables are included in the price of this booth. I've never needed more than two before but there are always last-minute changes. People overbook tables just in case and when they set up, they figure out they don't actually have room for them all. I was pretty sure I'd be able to find one. Thanks, guys," Kat called to the two men as they left. She looked at her watch. "We have half an hour until the doors open. I'm already set up, so if you're all right with chili, I can get us something to eat while you get organized."

Kat went off to find them dinner and Barb stood in the booth, staring at her supplies. This would be a far cry from the professional wrapping stations she was used to, where huge rolls of gift-wrap were stacked on industrial racks and shelves of assorted ribbons and bows were separated by colour.

She knew that people would want to choose their gift-wrap, so she placed a tall plastic bin on the floor and stood all of the rolls of paper on end in it. Then she dragged it to the far end of the booth and positioned it between her table and the front display.

Next, she put the rolls of ribbon in a smaller bin and set that on the table. Another bin held gift tags and a set of coloured markers for writing the names of the recipients.

The fancy trims, tassels, painted pine cones, and greenery she left in bags. Those were things that she decided to use or not use when she was wrapping. That was the *magic* part of her service, the final flourishes that elevated her gift-wrapping to another level.

Finally, she pulled out the tray that held her scissors, cutting knives, tapes, and glues. She had just set that at the end of her table when Kat returned.

"I look forward to this chili every year," she said, putting a plastic tray down on Barb's table. "The women's shelter makes it. It's the same recipe but because they have new people cooking each year, it's always just a little bit different. Grab one."

Barb took one of the Styrofoam bowls off the tray and lifted the lid. Spicy steam wafted up, and her stomach growled, a reminder that she'd forgotten to eat lunch. She tore the plastic off a spoon and dug in.

"This is really good," she said.

"Oh, and there's garlic bread." Kat passed her a waxed paper envelope.

They were quiet for the few moments it took to eat.

"Will it be busy first thing?" Barb asked. She still had to do some sample wrapping for Kat to display. She set her empty bowl on the tray and wiped garlic butter off her fingers. She'd need to wash her hands before she touched any gift-wrap.

"I'm usually busy," Kat said. She shrugged. "I have a bit of a following and everyone wants to see my new pieces."

"I better go clean up," Barb said. "If you can dig up a couple of boxes, I'll get them wrapped as soon as I can."

Barb took the tray and sorted the recyclables before heading to the washroom. Hands clean, she hurried back to the booth.

The doors must have opened because Kat had three customers eyeing her jewelry.

Two small boxes were on her table. She caught Kat's eye and nodded.

Then she got to work.

It was harder than she'd expected. She had one box almost wrapped, but she wasn't happy with it and she didn't know why. If she couldn't figure this out, her business would be finished before she even really got started.

Kat came over.

"Melissa here is buying this for her aunt." Kat showed her a lovely silver necklace with a series of bright coloured stones nestled in a box. "She wants it to be special."

Barb took the box and looked up at a middle-aged woman wearing a red cloth coat. A bright purple scarf hung loose around her neck.

"Hmm. Based on the gift, I take it your aunt likes colour?"

"Even more than me," Melissa said. "Colour is joy, she always says." Melissa smiled a sad smile. "She's losing her sight, so this might be the last Christmas gift of mine that she can actually see. I want to give her as much colour as I can."

"I know just what to do," Barb said. And just like that whatever had been blocking her ability to wrap a gift was gone. In less than five minutes, she handed an exquisitely wrapped gift to Melissa. The metallic violet paper was accentuated by lime green ribbon. She'd used purple marker to colour in a few random scales of two white-painted pine cones and fixed them onto the small package with a tiny purple polka-dotted bow.

"Those are some of her favourite colours," Melissa said. "She's going to love it. Thank you."

"You're very welcome. Oh," Barb said. "I forgot the gift card." She pulled out a card. "What name do you want on it?"

"That was gorgeous," Kat said when Melissa was gone. "And so personal."

"Yeah, you're right," Barb said. "Maybe that's why I'm not happy with this generic sample. I need to wrap a gift *for* someone." She held up the sample.

"That is pretty," Kat said. "But the one for Melissa's aunt was inspired. Oh, I have another customer."

"Inspired," Barb repeated. Is that what happened? She was inspired by either the gift giver or what she learned about the recipient? You could tell a lot about people by what they gave and to whom. She stared at the sample. What if she pretended it was for Kat?

And immediately she knew what she needed to do.

When she wrapped the second sample, she pretended it was for Mitch. Heavens knew she owed the two of them for all the help they'd given her.

When she was happy with the samples, she placed them on

the table in front of Kat.

"Ohh," a customer said. "You offer gift-wrapping as well?"

A few minutes later, Barb was busy wrapping, and there was a line-up of Kat's customers waiting for their purchases to be wrapped.

"Do I have to buy something here to get it wrapped?"

Barb looked up to see a girl standing at the table near her wrapping station. She looked about ten and was holding a tin with a picture of a cat on it.

"Not at all. Oh, I forgot to put up a price list. How does two dollars sound to you?" It was a small tin and something about the way the girl was holding it made Barb want to help her.

"All right," the girl replied. "I bought this for my cat Whiskers. It's catnip. Whiskers loves catnip. I'm hoping that if he knows I bought it for him he'll come home."

"Whiskers is missing?" Barb asked. "How long since he's been gone?" This girl's mother must be around here somewhere; should she wait for her to show up? Barb didn't want to take money from a child to wrap a gift for a pet that might be dead rather than missing.

"A week," the girl said. "He got out by accident and might not know what our house looks like from the outside. I'm going to put this in the window so he knows it's his home."

"I see." Barb was about to decline when suddenly she *knew* how to wrap this gift. She reached out and took the tin. "Will you trust me?" The girl nodded. "I'll do something that Whiskers will like." She wouldn't charge the girl, but she was so sad about her cat that Barb wanted to help even just a little.

A few minutes later, she handed the tin back. She'd wrapped it in brown craft paper and tied fuzzy pompoms and three silver bells to it with twine.

It jingled when the girl took it from her and she beamed at Barb. "Whiskers will love this."

"Lindsay, there you are." A woman hurried over, a small boy trailing her. "I was worried about you. Don't run off again."

"Sorry, Mom. I saw the perfect present for Whiskers and this lady wrapped it up special for him, see?" She held up the gift. "It has all his favourite things on it and I didn't even tell her. Whiskers will come home when he sees this."

The woman sighed. "I hope he does." She met Barb's eyes. "Thank you. She's done nothing but look for that cat since he got out of the house."

"I didn't mean to let him out," the little boy said. "And I said I'm sorry." He looked like he was about to cry.

The woman sighed again. "We all know how sorry you are. What do I owe you?" This was directed at Barb.

"No charge," Barb said. "Just let me know if it works. Oh, I forgot the gift card." She smiled at Lindsay. "So Whiskers knows that this is for him."

She grabbed a gift card and a silver marker and wrote *Whiskers* on it. She cut a piece of twine to tie the card on with, and when she turned back to the card, she frowned.

Mr. Coleridge was spelled out in silver and she'd swear it was her own handwriting. Except she hadn't written that name down. She didn't even know a Mr. Coleridge.

Puzzled, she pulled out a second gift card. After checking that both sides were blank, she wrote *Whiskers* again.

Did she blink? She didn't even blink and now the card said *Mr. Coleridge*. Barb picked up the gift card and turned it over. And dropped the card onto the table. The back also said *Mr. Coleridge* and she knew both sides had been blank and that she'd only written on one side.

And it was her handwriting!

"Is something wrong?" the woman asked. "We don't need a gift tag if that's the problem. You've done enough for us."

"It's not a problem," Barb said. "At least I don't think it is." She picked up the two gift tags and turned to face the family. "Do you by any chance know a Mr. Coleridge?" They were going to think she was crazy, but somehow, she *knew* she wouldn't be able to write any other name on the card for Whiskers' present.

"He lives a few doors down from us," the woman replied.

Barb's eyes widened. She didn't know the man from the gift card but they did.

"He's mean," Lindsay said. "He sits on his porch and yells at us kids when we ride our bikes past his house."

"He's old," the woman corrected. "And not in the best health." She turned to Barb. "I've never spoken to him, but I've noticed that he gets visits from the Victorian Order of Nurses. Why do you ask about Mr. Coleridge?"

Barb held up the two gift tags. "When I try to write down Whiskers' name, it comes out Mr. Coleridge."

"Does he have Whiskers?" Lindsay asked.

Barb shrugged. "I have no idea. But I am sorry. I can't seem to write a gift card for Whiskers."

"That's all right. Thank you for everything," the woman said. "Come on, let's get home."

"That was weird," Kat said.

"How much did you witness?"

"From just after you wrote the first card," Kat said. "You seemed shocked."

"No kidding." She held up the cards. "I saw myself write that cat's name twice. And somehow Mr. Coleridge's name is there three times."

"Like I said, weird. I assume that's never happened before?"

"Never." Barb looked past Kat to her sign. *Wrap-it-up Magic.* She shivered. What was happening?

"I have more customers," Kat said. "Let me know if anything else strange happens."

Nothing else bizarre happened in the two hours between seven and nine, when the fair closed. Barb wrote a name on a gift card, tacked it to the package, and handed it to her final customer. She tucked the five-dollar bill into the envelope she was using to hold her cash and sighed.

"That was way busier than I expected," she said when she joined Kat at her table.

There were still a few people wandering among the booths but some of the vendors were already packing up.

"It was a very good night for me," Kat said. "I have to thank you for gift-wrapping my customer's purchases. Half a dozen people made their buying decision when they saw someone else with a wrapped gift."

"Glad I could help." Barb flexed her hands. She'd been wrapping steadily for the past two hours and although she had a minor paper cut, overall she felt good about her evening. "Will it be as busy tomorrow?"

"Later in the afternoon, yes," Kat said. "But Saturday mornings are usually pretty quiet. Come on, let's go home, have a glass of wine, and count our money."

"That sounds good."

Barb tidied up her table but left all of her goods where they were. Because her jewelry was small and expensive, Kat boxed her stock up and left it in the security office. Then they split up and headed to their respective cars.

CHAPTER 3

KAT WAS ALREADY home by the time Barb parked her car and entered the house.

"I poured the wine already," Kat called out.

"Thanks." Barb kicked her shoes off, picked up the glass of wine from the kitchen island, and joined Kat in the living room.

Since inheriting the house, Kat had remodelled the kitchen, living, and dining rooms, converting them from the multiple tiny rooms of the 1950s to a modern open concept space. The bedrooms hadn't been updated; at least the one Barb was staying in hadn't been.

It was tiny by today's standards, with just enough room for the queen-sized bed, a small side table, and an antique dresser that had belonged to Kat's mother. But it had the best view in the entire house: it looked out onto a wooded area that led up to the escarpment.

Barb sat down in the chair across from Kat, pulled her envelope out of her purse, and put it on the coffee table. "I should have thought to buy a cash box," she said. "This is less than professional." She sipped her wine and relaxed. "This is nice. I feel like I accomplished something." A feeling she hadn't had in the months since Richard had left her to clean up his mess.

"It *is* nice," Kat said. "After Mom passed and Mitch moved out, it's been a little lonely here. And it's especially nice to have someone to talk to after an event. I'm always a little too keyed up to go straight to bed." She pulled out her phone. "I have a pretty good tally on sales on my credit card app. I just need to count up the cash. Oh, and I have an old cash box you can have if you want." She opened her cash box and started pulling bills out of it.

"Thanks." Barb slid all of the money out of her envelope and sorted the denominations. "Wow, I made almost a hundred and fifty dollars. That's way more than I expected." If she did the same or better on each of the next two days, she'd make a few hundred dollars in profit and still have plenty of wrapping supplies left. Every single dollar mattered to her right now.

"Especially since you didn't get paid for wrapping my customers' purchases," Kat said. "Now I don't feel so guilty. I did about twenty percent more sales than last year's Friday night, which is in part thanks to you."

"Win, win," Barb said. She sat back and took a sip of her wine. "That was weird with the gift for the missing cat though." She'd been too busy to think about the gift card and the name she did not remember writing, and now she wondered if it had really happened.

"Very weird," Kat agreed. "You're sure you didn't write that man's name down?"

"At the time I thought I was," Barb replied. "But I must have. What other explanation is there?" But no one had told her that man's name. She couldn't even remember it now, so how had she known?

"I can't think of one," Kat said.

"Me neither."

Kat stood up and stretched, then set her wine glass on the kitchen island. "I'm ready for bed. I'll see you in the morning."

"Good night," Barb said as Kat headed down the hall to her bedroom.

She pulled the crumpled gift cards from her jeans pocket and smoothed them out. *Mr. Coleridge* was spelled out in what she would swear was her handwriting. She flipped them over.

She could almost see it as possible that she'd heard the name and written it down, even twice. But she would never write on both sides of the tag. *Never.* She was too meticulous when she was wrapping gifts: everything had to be perfect.

So how had Mr. Coleridge's name gotten on both sides of this tag? And in her handwriting?

Half an hour later Barb still had no answer, so she had the last sip of her wine and headed to bed.

Barb and Kat were ready when the doors to the Christmas Fair opened. The first hour was slow, but just after eleven a crowd of grey-haired women thronged the halls.

"I think the buses from the retirement homes have arrived," their booth neighbour Anne said. "They look but don't buy a lot."

"An outing is an outing," Barb said. Ever since Richard had left her destitute, she'd thought a lot about what her old age would look like, and she was pretty sure she wouldn't have extra money to spend on expensive gifts. But it didn't mean she wouldn't want to experience the holiday season and go to a Christmas show and sale like this one.

A few women stopped in front of Kat's booth but they weren't looking at the jewelry. Instead, they picked up her wrapping samples.

"Is this your work?" one woman asked, holding up the necklace box. "It's very good."

"Thank you." Barb joined them. "I've always had a knack for wrapping gifts. Do you have anything you'd like me to wrap? On the house."

"Oh, do you mean it? I'll find something, even if it's an empty box. Would that be all right? I'd love to have something this pretty in my room."

"Sure. If a small box will do, my friend might have one to spare."

"Oh no, I would like a bigger box, if that's all right with you. I want to be able to see it from across the room. I'll go find one and be back in a few minutes, all right?"

"That will be fine. By the way, I'm Barb. What's your name?" Barb asked.

"It's Rachelle," the woman replied. "Thank you, Barb." Rachelle put down the sample gift, grabbed the handles of her walker, and spun it around.

"Thank you for being so kind," one of Rachelle's companions said. "Rachelle doesn't have any family left and her budget is very tight. But she just loves Christmas. A pretty package, even empty, will help her get through a very lonely time of year."

"I'm happy to help," Barb replied.

Kat brought a customer to her and for the next half hour Barb was busy wrapping gifts.

"If you have time, I found something to wrap."

Barb looked up to find Rachelle standing beside her current customer. What looked like a battered cardboard pie box sat in the basket of her walker.

"I'll just be a moment," Barb said to her. She finished tying the dark grey ribbon, then took her scissors and scraped one blade along the ribbon until it curled into a corkscrew.

"What name would you like on the tag?" she asked her customer. She wrote out Michael in bold, black script, handed the gift to the customer, and then turned to Rachelle.

"Do you trust me? I think you'll like the way I wrap it," she said to the older woman.

"Yes," Rachelle replied. "I'm very excited to see what you do."

Barb nodded but her mind was already spinning with plans for this box. She took it over to her table, and in a few minutes, she was done. It was an elegant but traditionally wrapped gift in shiny reds and greens. She searched through her ribbons until she found one she'd bought on the chance that she'd come across someone French. *Joyeux Noel* repeated in gold down the centre of the white ribbon. She hand-crafted a bow and fixed it to the gift, making sure the words were readable on the streamers of ribbon that descended from the bow.

She handed the package to Rachelle, who smiled.

"En français, bien," Rachelle said. "Merci. C'est trés jolie."

"You're welcome," Barb replied. "I'm glad you like it. Just let me write up a gift tag. Shall I put your name on it?"

"Please."

To Rachelle, Barb wrote in red before reaching for a piece of green tape. When she went to pick up the tag, she frowned.

Instead of *Rachelle*, the tag now said *rose window*. Not only had the words on the tag changed but they didn't even make sense. Was that supposed to be *Rose the widow*?

"Is there anything wrong?" Rachelle asked. "Shall I spell out my name?"

"It's not that," Barb said. She sighed. If this was the same as last night with that darn cat, she would not be able to write Rachelle's name on this gift tag. "Does *rose window* mean anything to you?"

"I don't think so," Rachelle replied.

"Does it mean the table in front of the rose garden window?" one of Rachelle's companions asked. She turned to Barb. "It's everyone's favourite table in the dining room. It's so popular that we have to take turns. I ate there on Thursday."

"I was there on Monday," Rachelle said.

"Isn't that the day you lost your mother's brooch?"

"You lost a brooch?" Barb asked and Rachelle nodded sadly. This was so weird. Lindsay, the girl from last night, had a lost a cat, and now Rachelle was missing a brooch. But what did the message on the tag mean? Was the brooch there by the rose garden window?

"Oh, hi!"

Barb turned to find the girl she'd just been thinking about standing in front of her.

"I just came in to tell you," Lindsay said. "We found Whiskers! And he was right where you said he'd be. At Mr. Coleridge's house. He thought Whiskers was a stray so he'd been looking after him. He didn't see my posters because he doesn't go out much, and when he does, he forgets his glasses and hearing aids. He's not mean at all, he's just lonely. Mom invited him over for Christmas dinner. I just wanted to thank you," Lindsay finished in a rush. "For telling me where to find Whiskers."

"You're welcome," Barb said, even though she wasn't sure she'd done anything. "I'm very glad that you found your cat."

"Me too," Lindsay replied. "I gotta go. If Mom gets a ticket, she'll be mad at me." Lindsay grinned and hurried off.

"You found her lost cat?" Rachelle asked. "How? And does this mean you can find my lost brooch?"

Could she? "I have no idea how, but the same thing happened last night with that girl and her lost cat," Barb said. "I wrapped a gift for that little girl's cat, and when I wrote the cat's name on the gift tag, it somehow changed to *Mr. Coleridge*. Which as she just said, is where the cat was found." She held out the gift tag that said *rose window*. "I think this might be a clue."

"Rose window," Rachelle read off the tag. "I'll ask the staff to take another look there when I get back to the home."

"Let me know if you find it." Barb handed the wrapped box to Rachelle, who set it in the basket of her walker.

"Oh, I'll do more than that," Rachelle said. "If you can find lost things, we'll all be back. Someone loses something pretty much every day." Rachelle and her friends laughed as they headed away from the booth.

"What's going on?" Kat asked.

"I have no idea," Barb replied. Was she really finding lost things? Why was this happening? And if it was, how did she even do it?

Just after noon, the crowds came and things didn't let up until the doors closed at six.

Nothing else strange happened when Barb wrapped gifts: every name she wrote on a gift tag stayed put. Which again made her question whether anything odd had happened after all.

"Let's go out for dinner," Kat said. "My treat. I can't stand the thought of cooking something at home."

"It would be nice to be waited on," Barb agreed. She hadn't been to a restaurant since Richard left. In part because she hadn't wanted to go anywhere she might be recognized, but she also couldn't afford to eat out. "Are you sure you're all right with paying?"

"It's the least I can do," Kat said. "Since you won't take anything for gift-wrapping my jewelry. I think today might be my very best sales day ever, and I know some of the sales were because of your wrapping. Where would you like to go?"

"Somewhere casual," Barb said. "I know! I haven't had Swiss Chalet's Festive Special this year." The meal was a tradition she'd had for years with her sons, although Richard had never been a fan. Too *pedestrian*, he'd said, which meant it wasn't fancy enough for him.

"Perfect. Let me just get my stuff boxed up and delivered to the security office, and then we can get out of here."

Kat was done in a few minutes and they headed for Barb's car. She'd driven them both today but Kat had paid for parking. Tomorrow they would both drive since they had to pack up and all of their supplies—along with the two of them—wouldn't fit into one car.

Kat gave her directions to the restaurant and soon they were seated inside. The waitress came by with menus they didn't need since they both knew they wanted the special: a quarter chicken dinner with white meat and fries.

"I saw that little girl come back," Kat said. "You really found her cat?"

"That's what she said," Barb replied. "But I have no idea how."

"Maybe it really is magic," Kat said. "It's never happened before?"

"I wouldn't be so shocked if it had," Barb said. Mind reading might be more likely than magic, but something was going on. "I've done a lot of gift-wrapping over the years and nothing like this has ever happened. It's just so strange. But it was just those two gift tags."

"There was another one?" Kat asked.

"Well, I don't know for sure, but the same thing happened when I wrapped a gift—an empty box actually—for this older woman. I wrote her name on the gift tag but when I was finished, it wasn't her name on the tag. Apparently, she lost a brooch and the gift tag might be a clue to where she can find it."

"So why those two?" Kat asked. "And not anyone else? You wrapped a lot of gifts today."

"I have no idea why them or even what the heck is happening."

"If it happens again, you should to try to figure out what you did," Kat said. "It might be an unexplainable ability, but if you can do it at will, it could be useful."

"I guess," Barb replied. She could certainly see a use. Who wouldn't want to be able to find lost items? But did she want to be the person people came to for that? The way a medium would charge people to speak to their loved ones who had passed away? Most people would think she was either ridiculous or a charlatan. She'd suffered from enough notoriety because of Richard's criminal behaviour, she wasn't sure she could handle any more.

The waitress arrived with their meal and Barb purposely kept the conversation light. But it was hard not to think about gift tags that somehow changed after she'd written on them.

CHAPTER 4

BARB POURED HERSELF a second cup of coffee and took it into the living room.

She'd had a terrible night: she hadn't been able to shut off the horrible memories of being hounded by news outlets. Right after Richard disappeared, paparazzi with cameras—she refused to call them press—started waiting outside the gates to the house and taking pictures and videos of her just trying to get through her days. And just when the worst of it had died down, formal charges had been laid against her husband and it had started all over again.

"You're up early."

Barb looked up from staring at her coffee cup to find Kat standing over her.

"I woke up and couldn't get back to sleep," Barb said. "The coffee is still hot."

"Thanks."

Kat rustled around in the kitchen, and a moment later, she joined Barb, coffee in hand.

"Did you tally up your take from yesterday?" Kat asked.

"Almost three hundred and fifty," Barb said. "And I am shocked by that amount."

"Just think what you could make if you set yourself up as the finder of lost things," Kat said. "And that's a business that doesn't depend on a holiday."

"I'm not even sure I did anything," Barb said.

"Sure you are," Kat replied. "I know you. You didn't sleep because you were thinking about how you *did* find that kid's lost cat."

Barb sighed. "You're right, but not in the way you think. What do you think reporters will do when they find out I'm doing something weird like this? I was so grateful to you for asking me to move here because then I could get away from that. Why would I want to do anything to call attention to me?"

"Because you can help people," Kat said. "And make a little money. I know you're worried about finances." Kat sighed. "Dick ruined you financially and left you with nothing, so you need to earn a living. This could be your way to do that."

"I have other skills," Barb said. "I've done tons of things for charities."

"I know you have," Kat replied gently. "But what you *don't* have is paid experience. Or solid references. How many of the people you volunteered with will be willing to vouch for you to an employer?"

Barb's shoulders sagged. She couldn't think of a single one. Many of the women she'd worked events with had been victims of Richard, and she could not imagine any manager of a charity giving a reference to the wife of an embezzler.

"Dick ruined that for you too," Kat said softly. "You are great at wrapping presents but that's a very seasonal thing. Once Christmas is over, that income stream is done until next year. Trust me, I know what I'm speaking of. I do seventy-five percent of my sales in November and December, and most of the rest is done just before Valentine's Day. You might have some luck on other major holidays, but there aren't as many fairs and events for vendors. And the ones that do exist are small."

"I *hate* Richard," Barb said. She felt like crying.

"That's the spirit," Kat said. "I hate him too." She paused. "You don't have to decide anything yet. There's a couple of more weekends of Christmas events where you can do your gift-wrapping and you *are not* allowed to wrap my clients for free. So, we'll see how much money you can make doing those. In the meantime, try to figure out how you did what you did. You can always operate using a made-up name so no one knows it's you. You can always wear a disguise."

"And have a crystal ball?" Barb asked. She laughed. "What we're talking about is so absurd that no one I used to know would believe it anyway. Maybe I'll just revert to my maiden name."

"The Amazing Babble Fabel?" Kat asked.

"That seems over the top even for something this weird," Barb replied. *Babble* was the nickname Kat had given her when they were ten, and Barb had started calling Kathleen Henderson *Kat* instead of Kathy.

"The Fabulous Fabel," Kat said. "That's a pretty good stage name. And over the top is what you're looking for, don't you think? I'm picturing a blonde wig and the biggest sunglasses you can find."

"Sounds ridiculous," Barb said. "It might just work. But I have no idea how I did anything I might possibly have done." She paused. "All right, I *know* what happened. Somehow the gift tag changed to a name that I never wrote on it. In what looked like *my* handwriting. But I don't know *how* to make it happen, which would be a requirement for a business."

"Try to figure it out," Kat said.

"I'll think about it," Barb said. And she would—because she couldn't seem to stop thinking about it.

Barb left earlier for the fair than she had to. She gave Kat the excuse that she wanted to deposit most of the cash she'd made in the bank, and she did. Every dollar counted, so there was no way she wanted to lose any of it or be tempted to splurge and buy something she didn't need.

But banking only took a few minutes. And though it was satisfying to see her account balance go up for once, it was also a very small amount in the scheme of things.

She'd be lucky to clear five hundred dollars this weekend after her expenses. And sure, she would have made more money if she wasn't wrapping Kat's clients' purchases for free, but Kat had paid for the booth. Barb had no idea what that cost but even charging for every single gift-wrap might not cover that expense, let alone allow her to make a profit.

So, Kat was right. She needed a different way to earn money. But did it have to be some weird supernatural thing?

She'd assumed she'd be able to use her formidable organizing and design skills to work as a party planner or maybe a home stager. But Kat had immediately seen the flaw that she herself hadn't wanted to look at.

Not one single person from her former life would give her a reference. And she couldn't even blame them. Who wanted to be associated with an embezzler? Jeez, even her own children didn't believe she'd been as clueless and unaware—as stupid—as she'd been.

"I hate you, Richard!" she yelled as she drove away from the bank.

How could he have done this to her! And how could she have allowed herself to become so dependent on him?

Over the years she'd read all the advice to women about how important it was to have your own money, just in case. Even in happy marriages a woman could be left in financial straits if her husband died and the will took a long time to be settled.

So, she'd actually done something to protect herself. Every month she set aside some of the household expenses in a savings account in just her name. She didn't tell Richard, she didn't tell her children, she didn't tell any of her social friends. She'd thought she'd safeguarded her future from Richard.

She'd been so very wrong. She'd never had a job that paid a wage, so every penny she'd diligently tucked away was considered the proceeds of crime. The police had seized her bank account along with every other thing of value that they could find. That included her clothing, almost all of her jewelry, the house and all of its contents, the cars. With a very few exceptions, everything worth anything was sold to cover the costs of the lawyers and to partially repay the victims.

And she didn't think it unreasonable, not really. But it left her with limited prospects for the future.

She was sixty-two years old, and since she had never had a paying job, she was only eligible for the Canada Pension Plan as Richard's wife. And he had to apply in order for her to get anything. Or die, but then she'd need proof of his death. She had no idea where he was, so neither scenario was even possible.

Old Age Security, the last bastion to ward off poverty, wasn't available until she turned sixty-five. And even then, it was such a small amount of money that she would have to hope Kat let her live with her for the rest of her life. What if she got sick? What if Kat got sick or worse, died and Barb had to find a place to live on her meagre government money?

She turned into the vendor parking lot for the Christmas Fair and showed her ID tag to the attendant.

She had to seriously consider becoming the finder of lost things. She didn't see any other options, so she had to figure out how to do it.

She turned her car off and sat for a few minutes. It had been less than a week since she'd been forced from her home. She had to believe that she could make some money, she had to.

So, she would. Even if it meant using an unexplainable, supernatural ability.

The morning was busy. Kat's sales were steady, and many of her customers took advantage of free gift-wrapping, but Barb had plenty of her own customers.

Rachelle stopped in front of her table just before noon.

"The staff found it right where you said it would be," the older woman said, lifting one side of her winter coat so Barb could see the glittering brooch that was pinned to her blouse. "Apparently it somehow got stuck under the carpet right under the window. The rose window. So, thank you."

"You're welcome," Barb replied.

"Some of the ladies want you to find things that they've lost too." Rachelle looked over her shoulder and nodded, and half a dozen women joined her. "Is that all right?"

"I can't promise anything," Barb replied. "And you'll have to wait while I take care of paying customers."

"Oh, I'll pay," one woman said. "Ten dollars. If you can't find it for me, at least I'll have tried everything."

"I was going to ask if you wanted lunch," Kat said. "But I see that you're busy. Paying customers for your help finding things?"

"It looks like it." Barb turned to the woman who had spoken. "I can't guarantee I'll be able to find what you've lost but I'll give it a shot. What is it that's missing?"

At least this group of women would give her a chance to test out any theories she might have. Lindsay had told her that Whiskers was missing, and the gift she'd wrapped had been for the cat, but she hadn't known about Rachelle's missing brooch until after she'd wrapped the box and tried to write her name on the tag.

But there had to be something in common, otherwise every time she wrapped a gift, she'd be finding something lost, wouldn't she?

"It's my senior's discount card for the drug store," the woman said. "I've looked everywhere for it."

"That's what you want found?" Rachelle asked. "I thought it was something important. Just get a new card."

"When was the last time you bought anything at the drugstore anyway?" a third woman asked.

"I don't go because I don't have the card," the first woman said. "And just because I didn't lose my mother's brooch doesn't mean this isn't important to me."

"What would you like wrapped?" Barb asked.

"Here, wrap this." She handed her a small box. "It's for my niece. She comes to visit once a month and everyone on the whole floor loves seeing a young woman."

"Susan's niece Suzanne is a lovely young woman," Rachelle said.

"She's practically named after me," Susan said. "I think something festive but elegant for the wrapping."

"I'll do my best." Barb took the box and wrapped it. She wrote *Suzanne* on the gift tag and then, well, that's what remained on it.

"I'm sorry," Barb said as she handed the gift to Susan. "I don't really know how to deliberately find things."

"Oh well." Susan handed her a ten-dollar bill. "Like I said, at least I know that I've tried everything."

Barb wrapped two more gifts and the names on the gift tags did not change either time. She couldn't even have a weird business doing this if she couldn't find things whenever she wanted to. When people were willing to pay her for the service.

"Let Lucy have a turn," Rachelle said. There were still three women waiting for Barb to wrap a gift but two stepped aside to allow a tiny woman to edge up to the front of the table. "Maybe it has to be something of real value. Sentimental value." Rachelle sent a look towards Susan. "And not some stupid discount card you can easily replace."

"What is it you're missing?" Barb asked Lucy.

"A framed picture of my late husband," Lucy said. "It was the last picture he ever sat still for." She handed Barb a silver, framed photo of herself. "It was a match to this one, so I hoped that if you could wrap this for me, you would find the one of him."

"I hope I can." Barb took the photo. "Do you trust me? I know exactly how to wrap this."

"Oh please, do what you think is best. That's what you did for Rachelle, isn't it?"

"It is," Rachelle replied. "You even asked me if I'd trust you."

"Did I?" Was that it? Did she have to ask for someone's trust? Or maybe she had to wrap a gift exactly the way she wanted to. She knew exactly how this gift should be wrapped, so the only thing to do was try. "Let's see if this works."

She quickly grabbed the paper she wanted, and in moments she was gluing three white-painted pine cones on the gift. She stepped back: it needed one more thing. Barb stared into the bag of what she thought of as the flourishes. Ah, that one. She pulled out a sprig of pine bough and glued it in an arc above the pine cones. She nodded, satisfied.

"Lucy, what's your husband's name?"

"Ernest."

Ernest, Barb wrote on the gift tag. She turned it over and grinned. She hadn't written on this side but there, in her handwriting, was the name *Charlie*. She held the gift tag up so Lucy could see it. "Who's Charlie?"

"Oh my," Lucy said. "Charlie is my great-grandson. He's two. Are you saying that he has my Ernest?"

"I think so," Barb replied.

"You need to call your granddaughter," Susan said. "And make sure she knows she's raising a kleptomaniac."

"I don't think he's a kleptomaniac," Lucy said. "And I hope he did take it. It's nice to think he wants a picture of his great-grandfather."

"So that's the trick," Rachelle said. "You ask someone if they trust you."

"Try me!" said the next women.

Sadly, that did not seem to be the trick. Even though Barb asked the last two women to trust her, the names on the gift tags didn't change.

"I'm sorry, ladies," Barb said. "But thank you for your help."

"It worked for two of us," Rachelle said. "That's enough for me to believe in your gift-wrapping magic. I'll look for you next year. We have to go find our bus."

"It's a van," Susan said. "And not very big but the centre insists on calling it a bus. It was fun even though it didn't work for me. And I believe in your magic too. It's that time of year."

The rest of them waved before they headed out into the crowd.

"I asked some customers to come back while you took care of them," Kat said, joining her. "And then I watched. You learned something."

"I did," Barb agreed. "I need to ask them to trust me to wrap their gift. But I think that the lost thing has to be very important to the person who lost it." She shrugged. "Or maybe the lost item has to be able to be found." It was entirely possible a pharmacy discount card had been found and thrown into the trash. Even her weird talent wouldn't send an old woman to the dump to look for something, would it?

"The cat, the brooch, and just now the picture," Kat said. "All three things are also irreplaceable."

"I guess they are." She shook her head. "This is going to be the strangest business ever." She looked up at the sign she'd made: *Wrap-it-up Magic*. Magic indeed.

A couple of Kat's customers returned and soon she was focused on wrapping gifts. She was busy until the doors closed. It took another hour before all of her things were packed up in her car. She yawned. "I'll meet you at home," she called out to Kat, who had some paperwork to complete to secure next year's booth rental.

Home, she thought as she got in her car. And a business, strange as it was. It was not the life she'd expected to be living, but she had hope. And after all she'd been through, that seemed an incredible feat.

CHAPTER 5

BARB ARRIVED HOME first and spent a few minutes tallying up her profits.

After subtracting all of her expenses, including parking, she'd cleared $635 during the Christmas Fair weekend. What made her even happier was that Kat said she'd had, by far, her best sales weekend ever and she credited Barb's free gift-wrapping with helping her do that. And having someone there who could cover for bathroom and meal breaks meant that Kat hadn't had to close down her shop even for a moment all weekend. Kat usually asked Mitch to drop in for a few minutes each day but her daughter wasn't always available. Non-staffed booths were not only frowned on by the event organizers but they potentially cost sales.

Barb was incredibly relieved that she wasn't starting off her stay at Kat's house as a complete burden. With the money she'd made, she could buy their groceries for the month of December and maybe January too. She definitely planned to pay for and cook Christmas dinner.

Plus, there were two more weekends of events lined up before Christmas. Profits from those should cover her gas and car insurance for the rest of the year, allowing her to forgo dipping into her meagre savings.

She'd been worried that her money would run out before she could earn anything, and here she was, already making a profit.

It wasn't a lot. When she thought back to her old life, this amount would barely pay for a months' worth of Richard's favourite scotch. But it was the first money she'd earned since she'd gotten married.

It was also the first time it was completely up to her how to spend money. Richard had always had a say in what she bought, even when it came to her clothes. Everything reflected on him, after all.

Barb was under no illusions though: she had to be extremely careful with her money and she would be spending on essentials only. But having complete control was both exhilarating and terrifying at the same time.

She'd thought she'd been a fully functional adult during her marriage, but now she realized that she'd given far too much of her autonomy and power to her husband. Not only had that inhibited her own growth and development as a person, it had allowed her husband to deceive her for decades.

She supposed it was better to grow up late in life than to never grow up at all. And she was grateful that she had a true friend who was willing to help her. Barb's task was to make sure Kat didn't end up poorer—emotionally or financially—for it.

"I picked up take out," Kat called from the front door. "Hope you don't mind burgers."

"I should have thought of that." Barb grabbed the bags of food from Kat. "Thanks."

"It will just take me a few minutes to bring my stuff in from the car," Kat said and disappeared back out the door.

Barb took the bags to the kitchen and got out plates. There was enough wine left over from Friday night for two small glasses, so she poured the wine and rinsed out the bottle. She'd take the empties back and buy more wine in the morning. She didn't want Kat to spend any more money on her sustenance for the next month.

The door from the garage opened, and Kat joined her in the kitchen, washing her hands before opening the bags.

"I got us both cheeseburgers and fries," Kat said. "Sorry about all the fast food this weekend. My schedule will be pretty erratic until after Christmas." Kat handed Barb a wrapped burger and a sleeve of fries before setting the same on a plate.

"Don't worry about it," Barb said. She pushed her glass and plate of food across the island and sat down in a bar stool. "But next time let me buy. I don't want you spending any more money on me."

Kat sat down next to her. "You know I don't mind."

"But I do. I made enough to pay for food so that's what I'm going to do." She unwrapped her burger and took a bite. She didn't eat fast food often in her old life but there was a reason it was so popular. It was delicious.

"So, you did all right?" Kat asked.

"Six hundred and thirty-five dollars," Barb replied. "I wasn't sure what I expected but that seems pretty good to me." When she'd volunteered for charities, someone else had always handled the money. She'd been privy to the overall fundraising totals but she'd never been told how much her gift-wrapping had raised.

"Especially since half your time was spent doing free gift-wrapping for me." Kat took a bite and chewed. "I haven't had a chance to figure out my total sales for the weekend, but based on what's left of my inventory, I did very well. I'll need to get busy and make more before this weekend's event. Are you going to do the finding-lost-things thing?"

"I was thinking of sticking to gift-wrapping, at least until I know exactly how to, you know, magically find lost things." Rachelle and her friends had been willing to take a chance while Barb tried to figure out how she did what she did, but many people would not be. She did not want the stress of disappointing people or worse, making them angry when she couldn't help them.

"You need to work on your persona anyway," Kat said.

"I suppose." Barb ate her last French fry and finished her wine. "I just threw all my stuff onto my bed, so I need to organize it before I can sleep. And I'm beat." She threw out the wrappers from her dinner and put her plate and wine glass in the dishwasher.

"You've had a big week," Kat said. "I won't be up long either. Good night."

"See you in the morning," Barb replied.

Once in her room she paused to survey the rolls of wrapping paper and bags of bows and flourishes. It *had* been a big week for her.

She'd left her old life behind and had made a really good start on a new one. She'd planned on buying the car and moving in with Kat. But starting a business? That was completely unexpected.

She sorted through her supplies, making notes in her phone about items she was low on. When everything was counted and organized, she sat down on the bed.

She was tired but still too keyed up to sleep. And she was nervous about her new abilities and the thought of trying to make money using them. It was so weird and had happened so suddenly that she wasn't sure it was smart to trust it. But what other choice did she have?

CHAPTER 6

BARB'S SECOND WEEK since being forced out of her home went by in a blur. She grocery shopped, picked up more wine, replenished her gift-wrapping supplies, cleaned the house, and planned and cooked dinner every night. It felt a little like her life before the police started investigating Richard's finances. Except for the fact that at the back of her mind she was trying to figure out how to earn a living with a very strange, unexplainable—supernatural—talent.

Kat spent her days holed up in her garage studio making more jewelry. Her sales had been so good that she didn't think she had enough stock for the upcoming event.

The Canadian Makers Christmas Show was being held in the convention centre for the next two weekends, and according to Kat, it would be almost as busy as the Christmas Fair. Everything sold at this show had to be made in Ontario, and Barb worried that her business wouldn't qualify.

It took a few phone calls but she finally spoke to the president of the organization. Gift-wrapping was a service and didn't have the same restrictions as the items for sale did. Barb decided to get into the spirit of it anyway. Many of her flourishes were from Ontario but she was able to source some cloth gift bags and fabric ends and even some locally printed gift-wrap. The gift-wrap was expensive but Kat assured her that people at this show would appreciate—and be willing to pay for—a locally designed and crafted option.

By Friday afternoon all she had to do was load up her car and set up at the venue. Poor Kat was still in her workshop frantically finishing a few of her more expensive pieces.

"Do you want me to take anything to the venue for you?" Barb asked through the open door. Kat was hunched over her table, the light shining on the worktable in front of her.

"Yes." Kat stood up and stretched. "Please. If you could get my sign hung up that would be wonderful. And could you take my display shelves over? I still need an hour or so to finish up here and after that I have to clean myself up." She gestured to her dirty overalls. "Although if there's an event where it's acceptable to look like a working artist, this one is it."

"Leave everything to me," Barb said. "I'll get us all set up so you can just show up with the sparkly things."

"Thanks, that will save me a ton of time. I'll help load up your car."

In less than fifteen minutes they had everything stowed in Barb's car. She picked up a final bag from the kitchen counter.

"I also packed us some sandwiches," Barb said to Kat, who was about to step back into her workshop. "We can eat whenever we have time."

"You're a genius," Kat said. "See you there."

"See you there."

It had started to snow, so Barb had to search for her brush and ice scraper. It was in the back seat, under a stack of Kat's displays, and it took her a few minutes to wrestle it out. Once the car was cleaned off, she tucked the brush on the floor on the passenger side and got in.

The fresh snow meant that the streets were slick, and it took her an extra ten minutes to get downtown to the convention centre.

Cars and trucks were lined up at the loading dock: vendors like her dropping off their supplies. But everything was well-organized. Event staff with dollies were on hand and vehicles were quickly unloaded. While their goods were wheeled inside, the vendors drove away to find permanent parking.

"Booth number?" a man asked when she made it to the dock.

"Thirty-two." Barb showed her vendor ID tag.

"All right. Tell us what's delicate and we'll get you unloaded."

In five minutes, everything from her car was stacked on a dolly. The man she'd spoken to slapped stickers with #32 on every visible surface. The dolly was rolled away before Barb even had time to get back into her car.

The vendor parking lot was already pretty full and she worried that Kat would have trouble finding a spot.

Once again, Kat's booth was front and centre. The dolly had already been unloaded, and everything from her car sat on the floor in the centre of the booth.

First things first. She needed to get the signs up, so she went off in search of someone with a step ladder.

Barb checked the time on her phone. The doors would open in fifteen minutes and Kat still wasn't here. Should she call her? She straightened a display shelf, hoping she'd set everything up the way Kat wanted.

Her own table was tucked off to the side and her Wrap-it-up Magic sign was pinned to the drape at the back of the booth.

"Where's Kat?"

Barb turned. A middle-aged woman stood in front of the booth, frowning.

"She's running a little late," Barb said. "Can I let her know that you're looking for her?"

"Nah, I'll come by later. Are you her employee? I've been telling her for years that she needed to hire someone. Three days without a break is not good for anyone, especially us older folks."

"We're partnering up this year," Barb replied. "And sharing the booth. I do gift-wrapping." Something about this woman put Barb on edge. She had a feeling that any advice she'd given to Kat had not been friendly.

"Magic gift-wrapping? Really?"

"So I've been told," Barb replied. "Oh see, there's Kat now."

Kat was rushing towards them, bags and plastic storage bins on the dolly that a young woman behind her was pushing.

"Oh great, you set everything up," Kat said. "Thanks so much. Sorry I'm so late. I think I got the last parking spot and it was a long walk." She turned to the young woman. "Right here is good, thanks." Between the two of them, Kat's goods were unloaded and stacked beside her booth.

"I wasn't sure where to put everything," Barb said as the woman wheeled the dolly away. "I hope it's all right." She had experience designing interiors but that was far different from designing to sell. She'd done her best to replicate Kat's display from last weekend but because she'd been preoccupied with her own set-up, she hadn't actually paid that much attention to it.

"I'm sure it'll be fine." Kat frowned when she looked at the older woman who was still standing in front of the booth. "If you don't mind, Magda, I have a lot to do and very little time to do it in."

"Sure, Kat," Magda said. "I'll come and check to see if you're actually ready for the opening. Although you might surprise me now that you have a partner."

"Tell me what to do," Barb said, ignoring Magda, whoever she was. Kat took the lids off the large bins and pushed them across the floor to Barb, who quickly took the smaller packages from the bins and laid them on the table in an orderly row.

As soon as half the bins were empty, Kat started unwrapping the individual jewelry pieces and arranging them on the display shelves.

Barb pushed the unpacked bins under the table to the back of the booth. With one last check to make sure her gift-wrapping table was ready, she watched Kat fill the last shelf.

"That was close," Kat said, stepping back to survey her display. "I could lose this booth next year if I'm not set up on time or my booth isn't displayed properly. So, thank you for doing everything."

"You're welcome." Barb joined her friend at the front of the table just as Magda returned.

"You made it," Magda sniffed. "But I'm not sure your display is up to par."

"Then it's a good thing you're not the judge of that," Kat replied. "Don't you have anything better to do?"

"As a matter of fact, I do," Magda replied. "The news never sleeps. Ta."

"The news?" Barb asked. "Is she a reporter?"

"She wishes," Kat said. "She writes a column in a local Facebook artisan group. She describes it as profiles of local artists, but in truth she mostly does hatchet jobs on anyone she doesn't consider a friend. She did one on me years ago and I did a fact-based rebuttal. She's been needling me ever since. My suggestion is to stay away from her."

"I will." Barb had no interest in tangling with the local busybody. The last thing she wanted was more scrutiny.

Barb took a quick look around at the other vendors just before the doors opened. She wanted to see what kinds of gifts she might be expected to wrap and figure out if the reusable bags she'd bought for the event were going to work.

The ambience at the Canadian Makers Christmas Show was very different from the Christmas Fair, although she recognized a few of the same vendors; people like Kat who made their own goods. What was for sale was very different as well. There were a lot more hand-crafted wooden items and original art along with knitted goods like socks and mittens. There was even one booth with handmade moccasins.

She saw people in security uniforms standing by the doors, so she hurried back to join Kat before they let customers in.

"See anything you like?" Kat asked.

"Lots," Barb replied. "But I'm not here to shop." She wanted to buy her sons Christmas gifts even though she couldn't afford to spend a lot on them. But their tastes didn't run to handmade gifts—especially not Rick. It had been so long since she'd spoken to them that she wasn't sure they would even accept gifts from her. Christmas was going to be really hard if she wasn't able to see them.

"The doors are open," Kat said. "Get ready."

Kat was busy from the moment people were allowed in to the venue, but Barb had time to eat the sandwich she'd packed. When she had a lull, Kat gratefully accepted hers and ate it standing up while customers browsed her display.

About an hour before closing time, Barb had a line-up of customers. Half of them simply wanted to buy the reusable gift bags, and she had to do some quick calculations to figure out pricing.

"I guess I miscalculated what would be in demand," she said to Kat when they had a brief break in customers.

"Can you get more bags for tomorrow?" Kat asked. "Saturday afternoon will be busy."

"I hope so. I'll have to visit the store where I bought these as soon as it opens." She didn't make as much money selling goods as she did when she used them as gift-wrap, especially since she was paying retail prices. If the cloth gift bags ended up being popular, she might want to sew them herself. Although she should start thinking of this as her temporary business, something to do just until she figured out how to make money finding lost things.

A minute later, both Barb and Kat had customers to deal with and the next half hour was steady.

Barb handed her customer a reusable gift bag, thanked her, and smiled at her next customer. The woman held up a bulky hand-knitted sweater.

"Do you have something that will fit this?" she asked. "My daughter doesn't want anything that's not environmentally friendly and made locally." She rolled her eyes. "Every gift has to have *provenance*. It makes her difficult to buy for."

"All children are difficult to buy for," Barb said. "Once they get to a certain age."

"They are much easier when they're younger," the woman agreed.

Barb eyed the sweater. She didn't think she had a cloth gift bag that it would fit into without crushing it, but she had an idea. "Will you trust me to wrap that?"

"Why not?" The woman carefully folded the sweater and

handed it to Barb.

Barb put it on her table and rooted through her supplies. She pulled out a length of burgundy cloth and instead of measuring the exact amount required, she cut a generous piece. Once the sweater was bundled up in the fabric, she tied it all with green twine and added a few sprigs of pine.

"I hope you like it," Barb said as she handed the bundle to her customer. "There's enough fabric that your daughter can use it to make something if she's crafty or she can donate it to someone else. Reduce and reuse, right?"

"And it looks lovely," the woman said. "I expected to be embarrassed to give her this gift but I'm happy to say that I won't be."

"I can make a gift card out of craft paper," Barb said. "If you think that's allowed. It can be recycled."

"Yes. Let me have one small thing that I consider normal. Her name is Natalie."

Barb took a small piece of craft paper and folded it to make a half bow with a longer flat edge. On the flat part she wrote *Natalie*. But when she looked at it, it said *Marty's Mart* in her handwriting.

"You've had something go missing recently, haven't you?" Barb asked her customer.

"I have," was the reply. "Why do you ask?"

"Because I think I know where it is." Barb held out the gift tag. "Do you know a place called Marty's Mart?"

"That's a pawn shop near my home," the woman answered. "Are you telling me that my vase is there? How would you know? How do you even know I'm missing anything?"

Barb pointed to her sign, *Wrap-it-up Magic*.

"Magic? Do you think I'm a fool? Here." The woman handed her a ten-dollar bill. "I'm not sure what you're up to, but I don't think it's funny." She took her wrapped gift and stormed off.

Barb frowned. After she'd helped Lindsay and Rachelle and her friends, she'd made an assumption that everyone would want her help. That was obviously very wrong. Next time she'd ask. Except she hadn't known she was going to find something for that customer. She paused. She *had* asked her to trust her.

A few minutes later the doors were locked. When Barb wrapped gifts for a couple of lingering shoppers, she deliberately did not ask them to trust her.

CHAPTER 7

"I STILL FIND it strange that someone was offended when you tried to help them find something they'd lost," Kat said.

"It hadn't crossed my mind either," Barb said and shrugged. It was Saturday morning and they were drinking coffee while they waited for the doors to open. "Not that I actually realized I was going to find a lost item. Not even when I asked her if she trusted me. Which, for the record, I will not say to anyone today."

"I don't think you should let one angry person stop you from trying to help people."

"I guess," Barb said. She still wasn't going to try to find any lost items today. The woman from the night before had been pretty angry. And dismissive about the possibility that Barb had used magic. Not that Barb could really blame her for that. She wasn't ready to call what she did magic, and she *knew* there was no other explanation for what she was doing.

Barb finished her coffee and tossed the empty cup in the garbage. "Looks like the doors are open."

"I'm ready," Kat said. "How about you?"

"Yep," Barb replied. She didn't have a choice; people were already starting to fill the aisles.

For the next few hours, business was steady for both Kat and Barb. It was a good thing Barb had been able to get out early and replenish her selection of cloth gift bags. She'd also bought more plain fabric so when she was actually asked to wrap presents, she had options for people to choose from. And she made sure she had *them* choose: no more asking customers to trust her to decide how to wrap an item. She didn't know exactly how her talent worked but so far that question was common in every single instance where the gift tag gave a clue to finding a lost item.

"There she is, Officer."

Barb looked up to find the angry woman from last night pointing at her, a uniformed police officer at her side. Barb froze at the sight of the cop. She'd had to deal with far too many of them after Richard disappeared.

"Ma'am," the police officer said. "Mrs. Cathcart here says that you knew her stolen vase was at the pawn shop."

"How would I know that?" Barb asked. She did not want to lie to the police officer but he would never believe the truth. She barely believed it herself.

"Exactly!" Mrs. Cathcart crowed. "How would you know where it was unless you or someone you know stole it?" She held up a small, blue patterned vase.

A crowd was starting to gather, and Barb's stomach knotted when she saw Magda the gossip edge closer.

"Can we speak somewhere more private?" Barb asked. "I don't want to disrupt my friend's sales. This is an important event for her." She nodded at Kat, who mouthed *can I help*? Barb shook her head.

"I bet she was in on it too," Mrs. Cathcart said. "I think you should arrest both of them."

"Mrs. Brown," the police officer said. "There is no proof that your vase was even stolen, let alone by this woman. Now, ma'am, can I see some ID?"

Barb grabbed her purse from under her wrapping table and pulled out her wallet. She passed her driver's license to the officer.

"Barbara Baker," he read out. "Is it Mrs. Baker?"

"Ms.," Barb replied. "I'm separated." She wished she'd changed her name on her ID to her maiden name. It would be so much better to have the police talk to Barbara Fabel instead of Barbara Baker, who was *known to police.*

"Ms. Baker, you do recognize Mrs. Cathcart, don't you?"

"Yes. She had me wrap a sweater for her daughter last night. I thought she was happy with what I did."

"I was, I am," Mrs. Cathcart said. "Until you started talking about Marty's Mart, telling me that's where I would find something that had gone missing. Which is exactly where I found my vase this morning."

"I have never been to this Marty's Mart," Barb replied. "And if I had anything to do with your vase being there, why would I tell you that's where it was?"

"So that you can pretend that you can do *magic.*" Mrs. Cathcart screwed up her face on that last word. "So that you can overcharge gullible people."

"Do you feel that I overcharged you? Is that what this is about?" Barb asked. "I'll refund you your ten dollars." She pulled a bill out of her wallet and held it out. She just wanted this to go away. She just wanted everyone to leave her alone.

"Mrs. Cathcart," the police office said. "Is that what this is really about?"

"No, it's about this woman pretending that knowing where my vase was is some kind of magic when the only way she could have known was if she was involved with its disappearance."

"Mrs. Cathcart, the shop owner said it was brought in by a young woman," the officer said. He turned to Barb. "Ms. Baker. I am not here to accuse you of anything, I just needed your confirmation that you had no idea that the vase was at the pawn shop." He handed her driver's license back to her. "The shop owner is sending me the security footage. Are you going to be on it?"

"No. I have never been to this store," Barb replied.

"Then I won't bother you again. Mrs. Cathcart, please come with me and let Ms. Baker get back to her work."

The cop steered Mrs. Cathcart through the crowd and Barb blew out a big breath.

"I need another coffee," she said to Kat. "Want one?"

Kat nodded and Barb practically ran away from the booth. She knew from experience that people didn't go away until the main focus—in this case her—was gone. She needed to escape that crowd just as much as she needed to have them leave poor Kat alone.

It was almost an hour before she felt calm enough to return to the booth. She was relieved to see that it was just Kat and her customers. Oh no, Magda Olsen was still hanging around. Barb did her best to ignore the woman as she entered the booth and handed Kat her coffee.

"Are you all right?" her friend asked.

"Sure," Barb lied. "I hope that didn't hurt your business."

"It might have actually helped," Kat said. "The crowd hung around for a few minutes and some of them took a look at my stuff while they waited. I made three sales."

"Good."

"Ms. Baker," Magda said. She had her phone in her hand no doubt ready to record whatever Barb said. "Would you care to comment on what happened here? That was quite an accusation that Mrs. Cathcart made. Do you know why she would say such things?"

"No comment," Barb replied. "I suggest you ask Mrs. Cathcart why she said that, or better yet, talk to that police officer."

"I plan to," Magda said. "I just thought I'd get your statement first. But if you don't want to tell me your side of the story, then I'll just have to figure it out on my own." She put her phone in her pocket and walked away from the booth.

"It's not a story," Barb said under her breath.

"She'll write what she wants to write no matter what you tell her," Kat said. "You were smart to ignore her."

"Smart, sure." But Barb didn't feel smart. She felt exposed, just like she'd felt when reporters had hounded her about Richard.

No one accused Barb of anything for the rest of the day, and thankfully, Mrs. Cathcart's accusation didn't have lingering effects on their sales: both Barb and Kat were busy. Nothing else strange happened, and what Barb wrote on the gift tags stayed on them, although one time she had to stop herself from asking a customer if he'd trust her.

Then she worried about what the man had lost that she could have helped him find. A memento from his wife perhaps, or something he cherished because it used to belong to his dead child.

She had to keep telling herself that it wasn't her job to find things other people had lost, but she never completely convinced herself.

The fact was that she could help people—she *wanted* to help people—and it was frustrating to hold herself back. She had no idea why or how she was doing it, but since she could, she felt terrible not using this ability to do good.

Finally, the doors closed, and she and Kat packed up and headed home.

Barb made them soup and sandwiches for dinner, and after counting up her money, she said good night to Kat and headed to her room.

She was exhausted but still too keyed up to sleep, so she pulled up Facebook and looked up Magda Olsen.

"Crap." Her heart sank: Magda had already posted an article about Barb's encounter with Mrs. Cathcart and the police. She'd called it *Do We Have a Thief Among Us?*

She read the first part of the post and relaxed. It seems that Magda had spoken to the police officer, who had evidence that Barb was not the person who had pawned the vase. It turned out that Natalie Cathcart, the daughter, was seen on security footage taking the vase into Marty's Mart and leaving without it.

"It would be nice if someone apologized," Barb said. At least she was in the clear. There was more to the article and she scrolled down.

And felt cold all over when she saw the picture of her and Richard, smiling as they arrived on the red carpet for the AGO Gala.

And there it was, the last half year or so of her life described with malevolent glee by a woman Barb didn't know but who felt justified in not only laying out the facts, but also quoting and linking to some of the most egregious articles that had been written about her.

Then Barb made the mistake of reading the comments. *Despicable thief* and *she should be run out of Hamilton* were some of the tamer comments.

She had to tell Kat. She had to warn her.

Barb took her phone out to the living room but Kat had already gone to her room. Rather than disturb her friend, Barb decided to wait until the morning. There was no way she could go back to the Christmas show tomorrow. She knew the circus that would be waiting for her and she was not interested in dealing with that.

And the last thing she wanted to do was ruin Kat's sales. This was an important time of year for her, and Barb did not want to repay her friend's kindness by costing her money.

If Barb didn't show up tomorrow, the press and Nosy Parkers would eventually leave. She hoped.

She put her phone in a drawer—there was no need to read every dreadful comment— turned off the light, and lay down.

But it was a long time before she was able to sleep.

CHAPTER 8

BARB WOKE UP early, and although she'd promised herself that she wouldn't, she read every single comment on Magda's story. There were a few people who seemed to have a more balanced view. In particular, a few were saying that it made no sense for someone who had embezzled millions to be working at the Canadian Makers Christmas Show, but for the most part, people said hateful things about her and wanted her gone.

When she'd read every single horrible, nasty comment, she left her room and made a pot of coffee. Kat would be up soon and she needed some caffeine before she told her that she'd ruined her life.

Barb had just poured her second cup of coffee when Kat come down the hallway.

"Ohh, you made coffee, excellent," Kat said. She poured a cup and brought it into the living room. "What's wrong?"

"Everything," Barb said. "I'm so sorry. Magda Olsen wrote about me and Richard."

"Did she write the truth or did she write lies?" Kat asked. "Don't answer that, I already know she wrote lies."

"She wrote innuendo," Barb said. "I was cleared of stealing the vase, but even the false accusation of one woman was enough for Magda to speculate that despite legions of forensic accountants finding no evidence, I must be a thief."

"Who stole the vase?"

"The woman's daughter," Barb replied. "She was caught on a security camera. According to Magda, the mother has asked the police to drop the case."

"I guess that's something," Kat said. "No doubt you *will not* get an apology from her—people like that never do the right thing."

"But this post of Magda's is going to cause you problems," Barb said.

"So? I can deal with Magda."

"You don't understand. People hate me. They'll hate you too and that could hurt your sales."

"Did you read the comments?" Kat asked. "*Never* read the comments. Most of those people don't even live around here. And the ones who do? I'd rather they didn't have nice things like my jewelry. Don't worry about it."

"I am worried about it," Barb said. "That's why I'm not going back to the craft show. It will be a circus but most of them will leave when I'm not there."

"Oh Babble, it won't be that bad, will it?" Kat asked. "It's not like Magda Olsen writes for a major newspaper—it's a local Facebook group with a few thousand members."

"It will be enough to bring out hateful people," Barb said. "And it might catch the eye of a reporter with a major newspaper. I'm going to stay home today. If you tell me that it's not bad, I'll rethink next weekend." She needed the money but not at the expense of her sanity. Or Kat's business. "I'll come by at the end of the day and get my stuff." Hopefully by that time, anyone hoping for a look at her would be gone.

"All right," Kat said. "I can't believe it will be all that bad though."

Barb picked up her phone: it was Kat. She'd left for the craft show an hour ago, had she forgotten something?

"Hey," Barb answered her phone.

"Just calling to let you know that you were right," Kat said.

"There was an ugly crowd here for the opening. Some of them even had signs. They're gone now. Worse though was the reporter and photographer from the *Observer*. They must have spoken to the event organizers because they knew my name. So don't answer the door if anyone drops by."

"Thanks for the warning. And I am so, so sorry about this." Ugh. She'd thought that she was done being trapped in her house because of reporters.

"It's Dick's fault, not yours," Kat said. "I'll call you later in case it's not safe for you to come and close up."

"All right." Barb ended the call. It *was* Richard's fault. Richard, who was no doubt living a carefree life that didn't include being hounded by the press while she was stuck in her friend's house all because he'd stolen money and then gone into hiding. At least if the press knew where he was, they could hound *him* for answers.

Barb sat up straight. That was it! She had this talent for finding lost things. She would use it to find her husband. She'd have to be careful how she leaked his whereabouts: if the courts and police found out the information came from her, they'd accuse her of lying to them. No one would believe she'd found him using magic or whatever this talent she had was.

She'd worry about that when she knew where he was.

Excited now, Barb went to her room. She had some gift-wrap and ribbon that she hadn't thought appropriate for the craft show.

It would be better if she had a real gift for Richard, she decided. What did she want to give him other than the finger? Or a piece of her mind?

Then she knew. Richard had ordered a bespoke suit from his tailor. He'd vanished before picking it up and paying for it, and for some reason, the courts had decided not to reimburse the tailor. Barb had sold her mother's pearls rather than leave the tailor unpaid. He'd been happy to see any money and had agreed to settle for the cost of the material—still thousands of dollars— and she'd kept the bill as proof of payment.

Now she would wrap it for Richard and find out where in the

world he was.

She tucked the tailor's bill into a small box, and with her wrapping supplies on the bed, she asked herself *will you trust me to wrap this?*

She nodded to herself, and then her eyes settled on a roll of wrapping paper and she knew exactly what to do.

Moments later the gift was wrapped, a black bow fixed to the upper left corner. She took a breath and selected a gift tag.

To Richard, she wrote on the tag in black script. Then she closed her eyes.

When she opened them, she grinned. It had worked!

Now the gift tag said *Montezuma*. She frowned. What did that mean? She pulled out her phone and did a search. Montezuma's Revenge came up but that didn't make any sense. Although she could only hope that he was suffering from diarrhea wherever he was. She scrolled down and saw a link to Montezuma City. She clicked the link. There was more than one city with that name but he would not be in Georgia, U.S.A.

Jackpot! There was a beachside city named Montezuma in Costa Rica, which translated into *rich coast*. Richard would totally choose to live on the rich coast, in part because he felt he deserved it and also as a way to thumb his nose at everyone he'd swindled. Including her.

Now that she was pretty sure she knew where he was, what should she do about it?

Barb decided that she'd get Kat's take on her next steps, so since she was deliberately ignoring Facebook and Madga's post, she spent a few hours reading everything on the web about Montezuma and Costa Rica.

What she learned only solidified her belief that her husband was there.

Costa Rica did not have a formal extradition treaty with Canada, which meant that forcing Richard back here to stand trial would be a difficult and lengthy ordeal.

She shook her head. That was not an accident: *Dick* always knew what he was doing and she suspected that this was no different. He'd probably had a shortlist of places to escape to. He might even have bought property in some of them. The forensic accountants hadn't found any overseas property bought in his name, but Dick—she was totally going to call him that from now on—could have had one or more of his many girlfriends buy a house for him. Her understanding was that if the ownership papers to transfer a property to him were filed overseas, Canada would not receive a record of it.

Her phone rang, and thinking it was Kat, she answered without checking to see who was calling.

"What the hell have you done now?"

"What? Who is this?"

"You've forgotten the sound of your son's voice already?"

"Rick? You're so angry that I didn't recognize you," Barb said. It wasn't her fault she hadn't spoken to her oldest son in months. He refused to answer the phone or return her calls. "What's wrong?"

"As if you don't know," Rick said. "A reporter called me this morning because somehow you got your name in the news again. You just can't stay out of the limelight, can you?"

"I'm sorry," Barb replied. Despite the fact that they'd been swindled by their father, her children had also been hounded by reporters. Although as victims they hadn't been pursued with the same intensity. "Something happened yesterday and a local busybody posted about me on Facebook. But she's not a real reporter."

"The guy who called me is," Rick said. "Now I have to keep a low profile because you are in the news again."

"I didn't do it on purpose," Barb said. Had Rick always spoken to her this way? It had been so long since he'd used a different tone that she wasn't sure. But the fact that she couldn't remember him being nice said something. "So be mad at the reporter, be mad at the busybody, but don't be mad at me."

"Oh right, because you're a victim too. No one believes that. *I* don't believe that. For Christ's sake you and Dad were almost on *Society Housewives of Toronto* because you wanted more exposure."

"That was your father, not me," Barb replied. "The contract was offered to him and his girlfriend, what's-her-face." Barb knew the woman's name but she preferred not to speak it. "The producers wanted to hire the cheating husband and girlfriend in the hopes of setting up a fight with me." That had been one of the most mortifying things she'd found out after Richard left. He'd been willing to be on a reality television show where his wife's public humiliation was a major storyline. It was near the end, when his Ponzi scheme was unravelling, so she could only surmise that he was hoping the notoriety produced more victims. But still, he'd been willing to do that to her for money.

"So you say," Rick replied.

"So the police say." Barb didn't bother trying to hide her anger. How dare he refuse to speak to her for months and then call up and blame her for terrible things his father had done *to her*. "I'm sorry a reporter called you. I didn't tell them to and the last thing I want is to be in the press. But it's not my fault. Take it up with your father."

"I would," Rick said. "Except I don't know where he is."

"Well neither do I," Barb lied. "I would love to talk to you, really talk to you, but if you're only going to call me when you're mad about dealing with the crap Richard Baker left for all of us, then I don't want to hear from you." She disconnected the call, wishing she had an old-fashioned phone where she could slam down the handset. She wanted to throw her cell phone but she couldn't afford to replace it if she broke it.

She paced the living room, fuming.

How dare Rick blame her for the *Housewives* horror. How *dare* he!

She wanted to call her son back and tell him where he could find his father just so Dick could have a taste of the hell she'd been living in for the past six months. But she wouldn't be able to explain how she knew where her husband was, so it would only make everyone think that she'd been part of the Ponzi scheme all along.

Now that her anger was fading, she was horrified that she'd yelled at Rick. She wanted to be part of his life again and her anger would not help her reconcile with him.

But months of her pleading with him to talk to her hadn't worked either. Let him be mad at her. She would mourn their strained relationship, but she was done letting the men in her life be horrible to her without bearing any consequences.

She sighed and sat down on the couch. It hurt but so had hoping he would call.

CHAPTER 9

"I'LL UNLOAD EVERYTHING," Barb said to Kat when she got out of her car. "It's the least I can do after the day you had. I already opened a bottle of wine."

"Thanks. I'm beat." Kat headed inside.

Barb opened the hatchback of Kat's car. Her wrapping supplies took up a lot of the space, adding to her guilt. Kat had called her an hour ago: Magda Olsen was hanging around so Kat thought it best if she packed up the booth herself. There was another weekend for this show so at least Kat had been able to leave her display cabinets at the venue.

Barb was grateful not to have to deal with Magda but felt guilty because Kat had. And if a reporter had called Rick, then it was more than likely one had visited the craft show.

It took two trips to get her wrapping supplies in. She simply piled it all on her bed; she'd sort it out later. There was a very good chance she wouldn't need them anyway. The business she'd been so excited about looked dead in the water. There was no way to conduct it when people felt that she was a juicy story.

She stacked Kat's bins of product near the door to her workshop. They seemed light which she hoped meant her friend had done well despite Barb's notoriety.

She locked the front door, hung up her coat, and headed to the living room.

Kat was on the couch with her feet up on the coffee table. Two wine glasses—one full and the other one half-empty—were on the table.

"Poured you some," Kat said. She sighed and sat up. "What a day. But you were right to stay away."

Barb picked up the full wine glass and took a sip. "Was it really bad?"

"The first hour was the worst," Kat said. "But as you expected, when they all finally understood that you weren't going to be there, they left. After that there was just Magda and some reporter for the *Observer*. He tried to give me his card, but I told them you would never call him, so he left. Oh, and that cop from yesterday came by. His card I did keep." She dug into her sweater pocket and handed the card to Barb. "He wanted to apologize in person and give you an update. But you already know what happened from Magda's post."

"An apology." Barb sat back in her chair. "I guess it's better than not getting one but his carelessness has upended my life." She picked up the card. *Constable David Moore*. She put the card on the table and set her wine glass down on top of it.

Kat started to laugh. "A coaster? You're using the cop's card as a coaster? Nice touch."

"He didn't impress me," Barb said. "I decided today that I was not going to let men get away with making my life miserable without some consequences." She shrugged. "But I'm not about to call this cop up and yell at him so . . . a coaster."

"That's a good decision," Kat said. "What brought that on?"

"Rick called," Barb said. "To yell at me for attracting the notice of the press. A reporter contacted him and it's my fault because according to him, I am looking for attention."

"Oh no. He blamed you? I hope you told him to get lost."

"I did yell back," Barb said. "Told him that I'd love to talk to him but to not bother calling if all he was going to do was blame me for the crappy things his father did."

"Ooh, good for you. What did he say?"

"I hung up on him," Barb replied. "I don't think I've ever hung up on my son before in my life. But he blamed me for the *Housewives* contract. Said that I wanted *exposure*."

"Oh, Barb, I'm sorry." Kat shook her head. "How can he not understand how absolutely horrifying that would have been for you?"

"And humiliating," Barb agreed. "It is anyway. The producers all know that Richard was willing to blindside me with news of his affair on television. I was told that Richard and what's-her-face's contracts were never signed because the producers needed to meet with me. Something Richard never arranged, probably because he knew I wouldn't agree to be on the show."

"I wouldn't mind yelling at Dick for a while," Kat said. "Too bad no one knows where he is."

Barb picked up her glass and grinned at her friend. "I know."

"What? How?"

"How did I know where that cat was? Or where Rachelle could find her lost brooch? I wrapped a gift for Richard and then wrote out a gift tag."

"Brilliant! So, where is he?"

"Montezuma, Costa Rica," Barb said. "It's a small city on the Pacific coast. A few thousand retired Americans live there, so I'm sure he blends right in."

"Can you find his actual address?" Kat asked. "Maybe try wrapping another present?"

"I never thought of that," Barb replied. "It's not like what I do has a rule book." She went to her bedroom and returned with wrapping supplies. But what to wrap for him? "I wrapped a bill I paid for him before but what should I wrap this time?"

"Your wedding ring," Kat said. "You want to return that to him, don't you?"

"Hell yes." Barb took off both her wedding and her engagement rings. "He can have them both. I'm not even sure why I'm still wearing them."

"Habit," Kat said. "But keep the one you can sell for the most money."

"I'll keep the engagement ring then." She wasn't actually going to send either ring to Richard but she didn't want to jinx the process. Besides, he would completely understand why she kept the engagement ring: he knew better than anyone the value of things.

She cut a small piece of wrapping paper, set it on the table, and placed her wedding band in the centre of it. "This seems very symbolic," she said to Kat. As she folded the paper and twisted it into a bow, she felt her shoulders relax. Once the ring was wrapped, she picked up a large gift tag. She closed her eyes thought *will I trust myself.* She nodded, opened her eyes, and wrote *Richard Baker, Montezuma, Costa Rica* on the tag.

When she leaned over the tag, she smiled and picked it up. "There are some more details. Casa de Cascadas, Cartt.," she read.

"If I remember correctly from a few vacations," Kat said, "*casa* means house, so his house has a name, not a number, and *cartt.* is short for *la carretera* which basically means road. So, he lives on Montezuma Road in a house called Casa de Cascadas."

Barb picked up her phone and searched for the word *cascadas*. "He lives near a tropical waterfall. Lucky him." She didn't even try to keep the bitterness out of her voice.

"Now that we have his address," Kat said. "We should tell someone."

"But who?"

"I have an idea."

"I was hoping you would," Barb replied. She wanted to think about Richard paying for what he'd done to her, their children, and all of his other victims. She did not want to think about him living in paradise complete with a lovely, tropical waterfall. At least she had hope that she could help change that.

"We need it cryptic," Kat said. "But also, specific. And above all anonymous."

Kat's phone was on the coffee table and Barb and Kat were huddled over it.

"That's exactly what the internet is good for," Mitch said over the speaker. "I'll throw in a conspiracy theory as well."

Kat's idea was to have her daughter reply to Magda Olsen's Facebook post with Richard's location. The hope was that if the press was monitoring the page, they would pick up on it and investigate."

"Isn't *this* a conspiracy theory?" Barb asked. "Won't too many conspiracies in one post look suspicious?"

Mitch's laugh echoed around the living room. "Only one conspiracy theory would look suspicious," she said. "I'll post a string of them but I'll keep coming back to where that ex of yours is living. How did you figure it out?"

"He mentioned it once," Barb lied. "And he's not my ex, at least not yet. We've never been to Costa Rica as a couple so I thought it would be good if someone could search for him there. But if the information comes from me the press will believe I was part of the Ponzi scheme." Some of the police officers she'd dealt with were sure she was part if it anyway: they just didn't have any proof. She was not interested in providing them with anything they could charge her with. Her future looked bleak but it was better than being in jail.

"All right. I'll get that done tonight. Thanks, Mom, I love this kind of thing."

"I know you do, honey," Kat replied. "If something else like this comes up, I'll let you know. Bye."

"So now we just wait for Mitch to post this?" Barb asked. "And no one will know it's her?" Her stomach was a giant knot now: this had to be anonymous.

"Mitch is good at this," Kat replied. "When she went to U of T, she volunteered at the Common Cause and did research into internet surveillance. She knows how to be fake on the internet. Besides, it's not like she'll be doing anything illegal."

"No, but there could be fallout if she's caught. I would hate for her to have the press after her. She runs a karate school. It's not like she can hide out for a few weeks."

"She won't get caught," Kat said. "And if she does, I expect her to take advantage of any exposure she gets."

"All right." Kat's assurances helped, but Barb still worried about bringing trouble to not just Kat, but Mitch as well.

"Let's eat and then we can watch Facebook for updates," Kat said.

It was after nine by the time they'd eaten. Barb was so nervous that she could only manage the soup part of their soup and a sandwich. Then she followed Kat to her bedroom, where she had her computer. She took her phone too: she had no idea how long it would take for Mitch's posts to be noticed, but she didn't think she would be able to patiently wait for Kat to read things.

"Ooh, the first one is good," Kat said. "Look for anything by user *iknowhatyoudid*."

Barb pulled up the post. "*Montezuma is no joke*," she read out loud. "*Criminals like Richard Baker have been hiding out in Costa Rica for decades. Rumour is that even Bernie Madoff had a place there. #PonziPlaybook.*" Barb grinned. "Nice hashtag."

"Oh, there's another one with the PonziPlaybook hashtag," Kat said. "But it's posted by a different user. I told you my daughter was good at this."

"*Montezuma, Costa Rica,*" Barb read. "*Hard to get to and hard to get someone out of there #PonziPlaybook #waterfall road.*"

Half a dozen more posts with those hashtags appeared. Then Kat chuckled. "It's been picked up by a real person," she said. "He posts here all the time and is a major conspiracy theorist with a lot of contacts."

"That's good, right?" Barb asked. "That means more people will see it." She felt a twinge of guilt for adding to the chaotic information on Facebook, but if it wasn't this conspiracy, it would probably be another one. And this wasn't even a conspiracy: Richard was actually where the posts said he was.

"That's very good," Kat agreed. "More people are picking up the hashtag. Oh look, Magda commented. She's asking for a source that she can verify."

"Will it stop now?" Barb needed a real journalist to be curious enough to follow up.

"I don't think so," Kat said. "Too many real people are reposting now. Oh, Magda just called out someone using the hashtag."

Barb pulled up the post on her phone. She recognized the

name. "That's a reporter from Toronto," she said. "Magda didn't waste any time."

"She's dying to work at a real news outlet," Kat said. "And since this is an actual true lead, this could even help her. I'd be a little sad about being responsible for legitimizing her."

"She'd stop being a busybody around here," Barb said. "So, it might actually work out better for me." She'd be more than happy to have Magda concentrate on real news instead of chasing her down.

"Glass half full," Kat said. "That's the spirit. I doubt the reporter will get back to Magda right away, and they will probably contact her privately. I'm going to say that's mission accomplished."

"Thanks for your help," Barb said. "I will definitely thank Mitch next time I see her."

Kat's phone rang. "That's her." She answered her phone. "You're on speaker and Barb's here."

"You are a genius!" Barb said. "It's already gotten to a reporter. That was so much faster than I expected."

"People are thirsty for new conspiracies," Mitch replied. "I'm sad it's over for me. That was fun! Tell me you need help with more things like this."

"We'll let you know," Kat said. "Thank you, daughter."

"My pleasure. Good night, Mom, Barb."

"Well," Barb said. "I'm going to bed. Thanks for the brilliant plan and your brilliant daughter's help."

"It all started with you finding out where Richard is," Kat said. "That's a useful talent."

"It is. Good night."

She headed across the hall to her room. It *was* a useful talent. If she could find Richard, she could probably find other missing people. Which meant she *should*.

It was time to get serious about her new business.

"You're sure you don't want to do any more gift-wrapping this year?" Kat asked. It was Friday and Kat was getting ready to head out to the last weekend of the Makers show.

Kat had spent most of the week in her workshop creating more jewelry while Barb had spent it searching the internet.

"It's too risky," Barb replied. "I haven't seen anything about Richard in the news but there have been half a dozen articles about me. So far not even Magda has publicized your relationship to me and I don't want to give her a reason to. Trust me, the last thing you want is a pack of reporters camped in front of your house. It makes regular life difficult and your neighbours hate you for something you have no control over." Even if she hadn't been forced out of her house, she would have moved and not just because she couldn't afford the property taxes.

Although to be fair, Richard had stolen from many of their neighbours, so they hated her for more than just the presence of the press. But reporters hanging around had made things worse.

"All right. After this weekend I have one more show to work. It's a full five days starting next Wednesday, so you'll be mostly on your own until Christmas."

"I can plan Christmas dinner," Barb said. "Will Mitch be coming?" She paused. She had no idea what holiday traditions Kat and her daughter had. "Or does she have you at her place?"

"Mitch cook?" Kat laughed. "She usually comes over around noon. We gave up on gifts for each other years ago, so she picks a movie and we eat junk food until it's time to eat dinner. After dinner we go for a walk down by the lake and burn some of it off. It's a simple day for us."

"That sounds lovely," Barb said. "Let me know if I'll be in the way."

Barb's Christmases were usually frenzied affairs. Richard always had business acquaintances over on Christmas Eve, then her sons came on Christmas Day, and to top it all off, Boxing Day was a drop-in open house for the neighbours.

For her the whole holiday period was days of prep and cooking and then the cleanup between events. And that was without including the work required for the gifts. Richard liked to make a show of presents, and Barb was tasked with buying and, of course, wrapping them all. Even the neighbours received small items.

She was sad that she would probably not be seeing her sons but she was relieved that she didn't have to spend hours in malls and stores that were crammed with people.

"You live here," Barb replied. "So, you're automatically included. And if you're willing to cook, I won't say no."

"Does Mitch eat turkey?"

"And gravy and mashed potatoes," Kat said. "If that's what you were planning."

"I'm happy to take requests," Barb said.

"I'll let Mitch know. Anyway, I have to go set up. See you after nine."

"I'll be here." She watched Kat get into her packed car and back down the driveway. Then she pulled out her phone and pulled up the Facebook app.

After a quick glance at Magda's feed, Barb went back to the page she'd found earlier in the day.

It was a Facebook page about a missing teenage girl. Seventeen-year-old Bethany Smith had fought with her parents three weeks ago, walked out of their Hamilton Mountain house, and hadn't been heard from since.

The page was filled with pleas to Beth to come home along with funny stories about the great times her friends and family had had with her.

Barb sighed. What to wrap for Beth Smith? More to the point, because she didn't want to venture out to buy anything, what did she already have that she could wrap for the girl?

She stood in the doorway to her room and looked at everything critically. She'd never consistently bought gifts for teenage girls but she had been buying for Rick's wife Margot for years. And even though it went against her gift-giving soul, her daughter-in-law always seemed happiest with gift cards. The last few years Barb had given her sizeable gift cards from Yorkdale Mall. It had pretty much every store you could think of including the high-end Holt Renfrew, a store she knew Margot liked.

So, she'd wrap up money for Beth Smith.

A few minutes later her home-made envelope was covered with silver stars and black ribbon. She wrote out *Bethany Smith* on the gift card.

When she picked it up it said *Mouse's house*. She frowned. What the hell did that mean? Was it a pet? A code? Or did Beth know someone with the nickname *Mouse*?

She scrolled through all of the posts on the Facebook page. Finally, she saw it. Someone had posted about Beth and the reply said *Mouse speaks or should I say SQUEAKS LOL*.

Was the girl hiding out at a friend's place? That was a terrible thing to do to her parents. Although maybe her parents weren't that great. Now she was second-guessing her decision to find Beth Smith. She knew from personal experience that not every home was a happy one.

She'd talk to Kat. This might be another task for Mitch to anonymously ask this Mouse if Beth was safe.

And that meant it was time to fill Mitch in on her talent.

CHAPTER 10

KAT WAS SO busy all weekend with the Makers show that it was Monday morning before Barb broached the subject of the missing girl.

"We need to call the police," Kat said. "Or her family. This girl's missing. Her parents must be going out of their minds. I can't imagine what I would have done if Mitch had disappeared."

"But what if her parents are the danger?" Barb had grown up in an unhealthy household, and she'd also spent some time this week researching missing teens. The results were heartbreaking: kids often ran away because they were being abused.

"That's not up to us," Kat said.

"I think it is," Barb said softly. "Because *I* found her. What if she is trying to get away from a terrible situation at home? I would be responsible for sending her back into danger. I don't think I can live with myself if she gets hurt because I made the wrong decision." Barb sighed. "But I also can't live with knowing I could be leaving her in a current unsafe situation. I want to tell Mitch what's happening and ask for her help. I've tried to search the person who was referred to as *Mouse* but their Facebook username does not seem to have any relationship with their real name. If Mitch can do the anonymous thing and find out more about Beth Smith's situation then we can make an informed decision."

"Sorry," Kat said. "Of course, you worry that she might be deliberately staying away from her home."

"I never ran away but I spent more time over here than at home," Barb replied. She'd never felt that her life was in danger but her father had been a firm believer in *spare the rod, spoil the child*. She married Richard to get away from him and in retrospect had traded being controlled by her father for being controlled by her husband.

"I'll ask Mitch to come for dinner tonight," Kat said. She picked up her phone and started typing. A moment later the phone pinged with an answering text.

"She wants to know if I'm cooking," Kat replied.

"I'll roast a chicken," Barb said. "Ask her what kind of potatoes she wants."

Kat typed into her phone and it pinged almost right away. "Either baked or mashed," Kat said. "She loves both. She'll be here just after six but she has to teach a class at eight."

"That should be enough time," Barb said. She'd make a list and go to the grocery store. She could even make a pie. She checked her watch. Although that might be a little too ambitious for the time she had.

"Great. I'll be in my workshop all day." Kat grinned. "It's a double-edged sword. Sales are really good, but apparently, I woefully underestimated how much inventory I needed this year."

"So, Magda's post didn't hurt you?" Barb asked. "That's a relief."

"It might even have helped," Kat replied. "You know, the no-press-is-bad-press thing. Anyway, I have stuff to make."

"I'll see you later," Barb said as Kat left for her workshop.

Barb pulled out her phone and headed to the kitchen. She opened the fridge; she'd check what was on hand and make a list of what she needed to buy.

It felt good to have a plan after days of worrying about what to do.

"Barb, that was fabulous," Mitch said. "Any time you feel like cooking, I am happy to come over and help you eat it."

"Glad you liked it," Barb said. "I am a pretty good cook. It's one of my few skills." She raised her eyes at Kat, who took the hint and stood up.

"Barb cooked so I'll clean up," Kat said. "And no, Mitch, I don't need your help."

"I'll just grab another cup of coffee," Mitch said. "The caffeine won't hurt since I have an eight o'clock class."

"Then you can join me in the living room," Barb said. "I'll tell you my ulterior motive for feeding you."

"Ooh, more Facebook sleuthing?" Mitch asked. Barb nodded. "I will be right there."

Barb headed to her room and picked up the envelope she'd wrapped for Bethany Smith as well as supplies to wrap something else. The best way to prove this to Mitch would be to show her.

Mitch was on the couch when she returned. Barb set everything down on the coffee table.

"So, I said that cooking was one of my few skills," Barb said. "Wrapping gifts is another. But since I moved in with your mom my wrapping skills seem to be . . . um . . . enhanced. In a weird way."

"All right," Mitch said. "Weird, I like weird."

"But only weird when I wrap a gift in a certain way, and I don't mean using specific paper or anything. I seem to need to ask the person to trust me to wrap the gift, and the gift has to be for someone who has lost something. Or is lost themselves. The gift tag I write ends up being a clue to where to find the lost thing."

"Wow. Is that how you knew Richard was in Costa Rica?" Mitch asked. "That is so cool."

"It's also how that whole Facebook fiasco started," Barb said. "I found a lost item for someone who accused me of stealing it. Before that I found a lost cat for a little girl and a family heirloom for a senior. I assumed everyone would be as happy as they were."

"This sounds like magic," Mitch said. "How do you do it?"

"I think I've figured out *how* to do it," Barb said. "But if you're asking *why* I can do this I have no idea." She shrugged. "And it sounds like magic to me too."

"Whatever you're doing, I'm in."

"Really? Without knowing anything else?"

"You want my help doing magic," Mitch replied. "I don't need to know more than that. And don't worry, I won't tell anyone."

"That's not an issue," Kat said joining them. "Barb is going to open up a business using this talent of hers. We're thinking some over-the-top costume and name. Like Zelda the Omniscient."

"Olivia the Omniscient," Mitch said. "Or maybe Octavia."

"How about Omega," Barb said. "It's Greek so maybe I can do a Greek gods theme." She could totally see herself dressing in a toga. "But right now, I need to know what happened to a missing local girl. I wrapped a gift for her and the gift tag said *Mouse's house*. I think I found Mouse on the Facebook thread." She paused. "But I don't know if she's hiding from danger or she's in danger right now."

"What's the girl's name?" Mitch asked in a serious voice.

"Bethany Smith," Barb replied.

"Bethany is a dead name," Mitch said. "One no longer in use. And they are fine."

"Mitch, you know this person?" Kat asked.

"I know Mouse," Mitch replied. "And I know *of* this person. They are safer where they are. They're only seventeen and returning to their parents would be very bad for them and potentially fatal." Mitch turned to Barb. "And Barb, the fact that you have this information is all the proof I need to know that you really can find lost people. Thank you for not immediately reaching out and notifying the parents. Why didn't you?"

"I married in order to get away from my father," Barb said. "So, I know that the happy family the outside world sees can disguise a lot of harmful dysfunction."

"Too true," Mitch said.

"How are you involved in this, Mitch?" Kat asked. "This person is a minor and has been reported as missing to the police, so I hope that doesn't make you complicit in some sort of crime."

"The cops, from what I know, understand the situation," Mitch said. "Hamilton has an LGBTQ underground. I never needed it because you accepted me when I came out to you."

"I accepted you before you came out to me," Kat said. "You being gay didn't change that. You're my child. People who don't accept their children for who they are seem to be more interested in how their child defines them than in being a real parent."

"So," Mitch said. "No Facebook fun for me. What's next? Find another missing person? Brainstorm Barb's new magical business? Oh, boo. I need to get to class." She stood up. "And Barb, I meant what I said. I'm available to eat any time you want to cook. Bye, Mom."

"Well," Barb said when Mitch had gone. "I feel like a weight has been lifted off my shoulders."

"It does tell us another thing about how your talent thing works," Kat said. "You found that person by using the name they no longer use for themselves."

"You're right," Barb said. "Maybe it's all about what I think they're called. I mean, I'm pretty sure no cat thinks of themselves as Whiskers, a cat I did find."

"Cats probably call themselves Fang or Killer," Kat said.

"Probably."

"Will you try to find another missing person?" Kat asked.

"Not a person," Barb replied. "At least not right away." She already knew what she was going to start with. "But this was a good reminder that I need to research my clients. Especially if they're looking for someone. Some people have good reasons to go missing."

CHAPTER 11

"I REGISTERED A new business," Barb said to Kat. It was the Monday after the final weekend of the Makers show and they'd just had breakfast. Kat didn't have any more sales events scheduled until the beginning of February, so Barb was hoping she had some time to help her figure out how to make her business work.

"Oh, did you decide on Omega the Omniscient?" Kat sipped her coffee.

"I decided that what I do is strange enough," Barb said. "I don't want to come across as a crackpot so I went basic. My company name is Lost and Found. And it's going to be completely online. I hope."

"Don't you need to wrap something for the person looking for the lost item?"

"I didn't for that one older woman Rachelle," Barb said. "I wrapped an empty box for her. I thought I'd concentrate on finding lost pets, so all I would need is some cat or dog treats to wrap. If that doesn't work, I'll rent a safety deposit box and have people send me something more personal." She'd thought a lot about it during the past week. Talking it out with Kat would hopefully uncover any issues she hadn't thought of. "Do you think Mitch could build me a website? I would totally pay her." She could hire someone else to do it but she didn't want any outside people to know who was behind her business. Although there were government records if anyone was that curious.

"Mitch has the skills to do that," Kat said. "You'll have to ask her if she has the time. Online only. I think that could work."

"Do you?" Barb asked. "I think so too, but I'm worried that I haven't thought of all the problems and pitfalls."

"I think lost pets is a good place to start," Kat said. "People who lose their pets are desperate. Where are you planning on advertising?"

"There's a website where people post lost and found pets. I thought I might start there. I could find a few for free and then maybe word of mouth would get me clients." Even if she didn't make any money for a while, it would give her something to do. She'd never really thought about her life having a purpose before, but she'd always been involved in charity work. She couldn't afford to give away all of her time, but she needed to be useful and she needed a reason to get up every day.

"So, what would you do?" Kat asked. "Walk me through it."

It took the rest of the morning but by lunch time Barb had a pretty good plan.

"Thanks for your help," she said to Kat. "I really appreciate it. I'll call Mitch this afternoon about a website but until I'm ready to advertise, I don't really need one."

Barb was excited because she was going to start finding lost pets this afternoon. She decided that she'd look for a local lost pet first and she'd just wrap an empty box. If that didn't work, she'd go to the pet store and buy some treats and wrap those.

"It's been fun," Kat said. "I'm excited for you. Even though this is the strangest business plan ever."

"Certainly not what I expected to be doing," Barb replied. "I thought gift-wrapping was an odd business and that's something normal. At least it is compared to this."

"Strange is always going to be more interesting than normal," Kat said. "Hopefully you can make this pay."

"Hopefully," Barb said. That was the challenge. If this business never made enough money for her to live on, she'd need to figure out something else. She'd only fallen into this because one of her few marketable skills was gift-wrapping. "I'll make lunch. I was thinking grilled cheese, is that okay?"

"With tomato soup?" Kat asked. "Sounds great."

Barb wrapped an empty box for a cat named Mr. Snuffles three times, and every gift tag she wrote out said Mr. Snuffles.

She'd have to try wrapping something Mr. Snuffles liked, but what? She reread the lost pet posting again. Male tabby, nine years old, lost the day before on the Mountain.

She assumed she could buy treats, but what if Mr. Snuffles didn't like the ones she bought? Would that matter? What had the girl bought for the cat she'd found? Right, catnip.

She searched catnip on the internet. Most, but not all, cats liked it. She'd buy some and maybe some of the more widely available treats and try again.

She grabbed her car keys and headed to the closest pet store.

The array of treats was overwhelming but she recognized a couple of brands that were household names and picked a few flavours: tuna, chicken, and mixed.

Thankfully there were fewer choices in the catnip section. She picked a tin because it would make a nice gift. Then because she didn't want to have to come back, she bought a few dog treats.

Back at home she wrapped the catnip, wrote *Mr. Snuffles* on the card, turned it over twice, and nodded. It looked like this cat like catnip.

The card now said *Francine Benoit*.

Barb pulled up the posting. She had to sign in—she'd used a free email account with her new business name for this—and replied to the posting telling them to check with Francine Benoit about Mr. Snuffles. She asked that they let her know and to send any other people looking for pets her way.

She sat back and blew out a big breath. One lost cat was not enough. She went to the next most recent, local lost pet: a cat named Bartholomeow.

This time she wrapped some treats. Sure enough, the writing on the gift tag changed. For a moment she wondered if Alba

Battlefield was a person but then she remembered that there was Battlefield Park was not far away, in Stoney Creek. She pulled up a map: when she found an intersection for Alba Street and Battlefield Drive, she hoped she wasn't sending them to find a pet dead after being hit by a car.

She replied to their posting anyway. She thought, and Kat had agreed, that every pet owner would want to know if their pet had died. It would be painful but at least they could stop looking and worrying.

Barb wrapped three more gifts and every single time the name tag gave her a clue.

Now all she had to do was hope at least one of them told her that they'd found their pet. And that they'd pass her email address on to others.

The tricky part would be what and when and how to charge. After reading all the lost pet postings, it seemed almost cruel to expect people to pay her. But she needed a viable business.

Maybe she should have focused on lost things that weren't alive? She'd have less concern about charging to find rings and brooches or lost lottery tickets.

But that might be more complicated. So far, the pet gifts were all generic: finding things that were valued by people might require something more specific.

After breakfast the next morning, Kat headed to her studio and Barb opened her email.

Three messages about lost pets! And they were all positive. Every single one had found their pet, even the one she'd worried had been hit by a car.

And even better, two of them wanted to send her reward money! She would accept it, of course. She spent the rest of the morning figuring out how to get money sent to her and still stay anonymous—she settled on an online payment portal that she could tie into her business bank account—and then emailed the information to the people offering rewards. It wasn't much, a total of fifty dollars, and she'd spent half that on things to wrap, but it was a start.

She had two new emails: two more lost pets, this time from people who had been sent her name by the successful clients. She decided she would call them clients even though they hadn't formally hired her.

The dog lost in Guelph was easy. The gift tag for Scooter said *Royal City* and her online search result said there was a park there. She quickly sent off an email telling the owner where to look.

But she couldn't find the cat. She wrapped every single cat item she had, and every time the gift tags continued to show the cat's name, *Purr Reginald Fluffypants*.

Maybe this cat was dead? Maybe it was too fussy for the things she was wrapping?

Or maybe it wasn't lost at all?

She replied to the email asking for more information about the cat: what were its favourite treats and where did it like to sleep.

She received an immediate reply apologizing for the trouble: the cat was safe. It belonged to a daughter who had broken up with her boyfriend, and the two had decided to share custody. The person who had thought it missing simply hadn't known about the agreement.

Barb sat back. Her gift or talent or skill seemed to know when something wasn't really lost. Interesting. She *had* found Richard, so what did that mean?

It meant the same as before: she had no idea how any of this worked or why. But it seemed to be accurate. At least when it did work.

She'd have to build that into her agreement with people. Maybe charge them for the effort—after all, she was offering a service that took her time and some supplies no matter the outcome—but without any guarantees. Would that make her seem like a fake? Would it make people angry at her?

"Ready for lunch?" Kat asked from the kitchen.

"Sure." Barb stood up and stretched. She should buy herself a computer so she didn't have to squint at her phone for hours. "I found a few lost pets and knew that another one wasn't even lost."

"Oh, that's a good skill to have," Kat replied. "To know if

something *isn't* missing. I'm pretty sure divorce lawyers would pay you for that kind of information. It would let them know if someone had disclosed all of their assets. If not, you could tell them where to look."

"Oh." Barb stopped in shock. "What if I could find the money Richard stole? Why didn't I think of this before? I found him so I should be able to find his money. Even if it doesn't work, I need to try." To be able to make amends, even in a small way and even if no one could know she'd done it, would make her feel so much better. She would consider that a bonus if it kept Richard poorer.

"I wonder what kinds of details you can discover," Kat said. "Can you find banks and account numbers?"

"I'm going to find out," Barb replied. Should she wrap a gift for her husband or for a victim? Maybe both. She'd start with Richard and her sons since she knew them the best.

During lunch Kat said things and Barb replied but she had no idea what they talked about. Her mind was racing with ideas of what to wrap in order to find the money her husband had stolen from so many people, including their sons.

At the mall, Barb stared at the list of stores. There were only a couple of stores where Richard and her son Rick would shop—and boy, at this moment was she ever aware of how snobby that had always been—but they were expensive, so she wasn't sure she should buy anything in those stores. Kyle had always been easier to buy for, so she wasn't as worried about his gift. But even though she really, really wanted to recover some of what Richard had stolen, she could not afford to spend a lot of money.

She settled on a silk tie for Richard, silver cuff links for Rick, and a bicycle pump for Kyle. The total was over four hundred dollars, and Richard and Rick's gifts would have been considered stocking stuffers for previous Christmases. Now the cash outlay made her anxious.

It was more than half of the entire amount of the money she'd made wrapping gifts; money she'd planned on using to pay for essentials so she didn't have to dip into her meagre bank account until after Christmas.

But if it allowed her to find some of Richard's stolen money, it was a price she had to pay. He obviously felt no guilt over what he'd done and how he'd financed their extravagant lifestyle, but she sure did.

Back at home she laid everything out on her bed: gifts, wrapping paper, ribbons, and flourishes.

Whose gift to wrap first?

"I'm going to trust myself," Barb whispered. She closed her eyes, and when she opened them, her gaze fell on the bicycle pump.

It would be awkward to wrap but when she'd wrapped gifts for charity, she'd always been given the hard-to-wrap items. She picked a blue patterned paper since blue had always been Kyle's favourite colour. After folding the paper into a diamond shape to cover the pump, she glued a couple of white painted pine cones to the top. She curled some white ribbon and trailed them down from the pine cones.

When she was done, she stepped away to look at it. Kyle would have liked both the gift and the wrapping job. She sighed sadly.

Christmas was less than two weeks away, and she doubted she would see either of her sons this year. Maybe she could drop this off for him? His condo had a concierge she could leave it with. She'd do it, she decided. He didn't even have to see her.

She picked up a gift tag and wrote out *To Kyle, always in my heart*. She closed her eyes and when she opened them the words on the tag had changed. But to what?

"BNCR Elliot Baker," she read out loud. The Elliot Baker part she understood. Richard was obviously using his middle name, but she was surprised that he was using his real last name. Was he hiding in plain sight or hadn't he been able to get fake ID? TV shows made that look easy but maybe it wasn't.

She picked up her phone and searched *BNCR Costa Rica* because she couldn't see her husband keeping his money anywhere except in the country where he was living.

Banco Nacional de Costa Rica: that's where at least some of the money Richard had stolen was. And under a name that was easily traced to him. Maybe it didn't matter? Maybe there was no way for Canadian law enforcement to gain access or freeze his account?

Rick's present yielded similar results except the money was in BCR: Banco de Costa Rica. But it was under the same name.

She turned to Richard's present, thinking that this time she would find an assumed name. Or maybe the name of someone who could be traced to a property in Montezuma.

Nope. This time there were two lines of script. One for BNCR and one for BCR and beside each was a string of numbers. They had to be bank account numbers.

"Kat!" she called. She pulled the gift tags from the three gifts and headed out into the hall. "Kat! I think I found it."

"What?" Kat stepped in from her workshop. "You found what?"

"I found Richard's money," she said. "I have what I'm pretty sure are his bank account numbers."

"I think you should tell the police," Kat said for what seemed to Barb like the thousandth time.

"So you've said," Barb replied. "I'm just not sure that's the right answer. I mean, I want the money recovered but I think I should give my sons a heads-up." She really wanted to contact Richard but even she knew that would just give him time to move the money. Although she could just find it again. But if that's what she thought would happen, then why did she want to tell him she knew where both he and his money were?

"Mom?"

"Oh good," Kat said. "Mitch is here. Grab a glass," she called out. "It's a wine night."

"Is that good or bad?" Mitch said a moment later when she entered the living room, a glass of red in her hand. "What's up? It sounded urgent."

"Sorry," Barb said. "I'm not sure it's urgent but I need your help."

"We need your *advice*," Kat said. "I am not letting you talk my daughter into doing anything illegal. Especially if it's breaking international law."

"We don't know that," Barb replied. She looked at Mitch. "It would be more Facebook work. I figured out where Richard is keeping his money, and I was thinking you could help me contact him and . . . I don't know, maybe I can talk him into doing the right thing."

Mitch sat down on the couch beside Kat and raised her eyebrows.

"You think a man who spent his life stealing millions of dollars from everyone he knew and then fled the country when the truth was coming out, will do the right thing?" Mitch raised her glass to her mother. "This might not be strong enough for this intervention."

"Is that what you think this is?" Barb asked. "An intervention? I'm not addicted to anything."

"Aren't you?" Kat asked softly. "After what Richard did to you; after all of the other women and embezzling from everyone who might be able to help you, he left you to deal with the mess he made. And you still want to give him the benefit of the doubt; you still somehow believe he is the kind of man who will make things right. It's either delusion or addiction."

Barb sat back in the chair. Kat and Mitch were right—there was no way Richard would be willing to atone for his actions. He fled the country because he wasn't interested in doing exactly that. He wasn't going to apologize, or take responsibility or return any of the money. So why did she think he would? Maybe it was an addiction?

"You're right," Barb said. "I think I am addicted. Not to Richard but to not having to admit that the life I lived for forty years was such a lie. To not having to admit that I was so oblivious to every bad thing he was doing that my husband was able to make me believe he was a good man. When in reality, for our entire marriage, he was a thief who was stealing from our friends and neighbours while I cooked them fancy dinners. That he *used me* to help him steal from people I considered friends and who he probably only considered marks."

Barb sighed. "I guess I'm also addicted to not allowing myself to be so very, very angry about what he did to me. Because if I allowed that, if I acknowledged all of that, then I would have to admit that my life has been worse than a waste, that I've been nothing more than a tool for my husband's thieving." She frowned. "I guess I've just admitted that."

Barb wanted to cry, she wanted to crawl into bed and just never get up. How could she have been so blind? She'd felt stupid after Richard left but now, she felt useless. She took a big gulp of wine. Mitch might be right; wine might not be strong enough.

"I'll get the whiskey," Mitch said as though she'd read Barb's mind.

While Mitch went to the kitchen, Kat leaned across the coffee table.

"Are you all right?" she asked. "I mean I know you *will be* all right, but how are you doing right this minute?"

"I'm not sure," Barb replied. She closed her eyes. How was she doing? "I'm furious," she said. "I'm mad at myself for not seeing what Richard was doing but I am absolutely furious at him." She opened her eyes. "I think this is the first time I've blamed him more than I've blamed myself. *He did this to me.*" A weight that she hadn't even realized she was carrying had lifted off her shoulders. Richard's actions were the root of everything. Her compliance and lack of interest in how he made his money would not have mattered if he hadn't been a lying, cheating thief.

Mitch handed her a glass, and she took a sip, the whiskey tingling on its way down her throat.

"And your life has not been a waste," Kat said. "You've volunteered thousands of hours to charities your whole life. That is not a waste, that's work. And as far as Richard using you? That's on him."

"I agree," Mitch said. "Richard is the jerk and charity work is *work*."

"It felt like work at the time," Barb said. She felt calm, like a storm had passed. The anger at her husband was still there but she thought she might be on the path to forgiving herself. "I'll tell the police where Richard and his money are," she said. "But it has to be done anonymously. If the information is traced back to me, the police will see it as proof that I knew all along."

"I can help with that," Mitch said.

"Thank you," Barb said. "But I need to talk to my sons first. I will not blindside them the way their father did."

"I need a day to figure out who to tell and how anyway," Mitch said. "Can I come over again tomorrow night?"

"Can you make it for dinner?" Barb asked. She looked over at Kat, who nodded.

"I told you before," Mitch said. "I'm here any time you're willing to cook."

"Text me your favourite dish," Barb said. "I can pick up the ingredients in the morning." Planning a special meal would help her think through exactly what she wanted to say to her sons. She wasn't about to tell them she had magically found their father and his stolen money, but she didn't want them to think she'd known everything all along.

CHAPTER 12

MITCH TEXTED HER dinner request early the next day, so Barb was able to visit the butcher just after they opened. Nicely aged roast in hand, she headed to the grocery store for a few more ingredients to round out the meal of roast beef and Yorkshire pudding.

When she got back to Kat's, she dropped her groceries in the kitchen and knocked on the studio door. Kat was doing her year-end inventory of both jewelry and supplies so she could figure out what she needed and order it in well before Valentine's Day.

"Mitch asked for roast beef and Yorkshire pudding," Barb said when Kat looked up from her work table.

"Of course, she did," Kat said with a grin. "It's something I've never made, but every Christmas Mitch wonders if we should have that instead of turkey."

"In my mind turkey wins out at Christmas," Barb said.

"That's why I've never made roast beef and Yorkshire pudding," Kat replied. "Have you figured out what to do about your kids?"

"They don't answer my calls," Barb said. "So, I'm going to text them that I found a brochure from a travel agent with Montezuma, Costa Rica circled. I'll say that Richard and I have never been there and had no plans to go, so I'm going to anonymously send this information to the authorities in case that's where he is."

"Maybe one or both of them will call," Kat said. "Once they understand that you really weren't part of it."

"I'm not counting on it," Barb replied. "Especially after that last call with Rick." She still couldn't believe her own son had accused her of wanting publicity. It hurt, especially since he seemed to have no idea how devastated she was. Richard had abandoned her but before that he'd planned to humiliate her on television. Why would anyone think that was something she wanted?

She fussed with her meal prep but once she put the roast in the oven, she had no more excuses. She created a detailed text and sent it to both of her sons saying that she thought Richard was in Costa Rica and why.

She really didn't expect to hear from either of them, so the next step was to see if Mitch had come up with a way to contact the police or the RCMP or whoever could track Richard down.

"That was delicious," Mitch said. She put her empty plate in the sink. "Thank you for indulging me. I half expected you to say no. It was a pretty big favour to ask."

"We're doing a trade," Barb replied. "So, it's not a favour. And I'm glad you enjoyed dinner. It's always nice to feed people who appreciate the work that goes into a meal." Richard's appreciation of her cooking early in their marriage had fuelled her passion to be an accomplished cook, but it had been a long time since he'd complimented her.

"I'll tidy up and make coffee," Kat said. "You two figure out what you're going to do next."

"All right." Barb grabbed her phone and headed to the living room. She put her phone on the coffee table and stared at it. No response from either of her sons. She hadn't expected anything, but she had hoped.

Mitch sat across from her. "We can always do one of those Crime Stoppers calls," she said. "I can find a phone booth and place the call from there."

"Phone booths still exist?" Barb asked. "Would you call the local police?"

"Toronto handled the investigation," Mitch replied. "I'll call them."

"That might work," Barb replied. "We'd need to give them all the banking information." Her phone rang. The number was blocked, and she almost didn't answer, but in case it was one of her sons, she picked it up.

"Hello?"

"Barbara, what the hell are you doing?" asked a familiar voice.

"Richard? Where are you?"

"Apparently you already know," Richard replied. "I don't know how because I'm certain there is no travel brochure."

Barb's jaw dropped. There was only one way Richard could know about that. "The boys have known where you were all along!"

"Not Kyle," Richard said. "He takes after his mother and can't be trusted not to tell the cops."

"It was Rick!" Her shock was wearing off and now she was getting angry. "All the times he blamed me for attracting attention. *How dare he?* How dare he yell at me when you were the one who left such a horrible mess?"

"Oh, calm down, Barbara," Richard said. "If you care about Rick, you will stop whatever you're doing. Stop trying to find me, stop trying to interfere. Rick's situation won't hold up to much more scrutiny."

"What do you mean?" Barb asked, but then she knew. "Rick was in on everything. That's what this call is about."

"He wasn't in on everything," Richard said. "Just a couple of deals in the last few years. But it's enough to send him to prison if the investigation starts looking at him more closely."

"You bastard," Barb said. "Turning our son into a criminal. How could you?"

"I didn't have to force him if that's what you're implying," Richard said. "He figured out what I was doing and wanted in. He said it was the only way he could afford to buy that house."

"You told me you loaned him the money." How many lies had

she believed?

"I couldn't tell you the truth, could I? Anyway, water under the bridge and all that. I need you to promise to keep anything you know about my whereabouts to yourself. It could end up badly for Rick."

"It is not 'water under the bridge'," she said. "Not for me. What about the way things ended up badly for me? I guess no one cares?"

"It's not like you're going to prison," Richard said.

"*You bastard!*" Barb yelled into the phone. "At least in prison I'd have room and board. I'm looking at abject poverty for the next twenty years thanks to you. I don't owe you anything."

"Think about Rick," Richard said. "He'll end up hating you."

"He already hates me." Barb replied. Her husband and son had sacrificed her and her future for their financial gain.

"He'll hate you more," Richard replied.

"Then it won't matter what I do." Her anger was starting to turn into grief. She would not give Richard the satisfaction of knowing he'd caused that. But she could scare him; cause him at least a tiny fraction of the worry and stress she'd endured in the past months. "You know what else won't matter? You leaving Montezuma and running somewhere else. I'll find you wherever you are."

"I'll have Rick give you some money," Richard said. "If that's what this is about."

"It's always about money for you, isn't it," Barb replied.

"You knew that when you married me."

"I did," Barb agreed. "Just as you know for me it's *not* about money. It's about all the lies you told me, all the false things you had me believe. My whole adult life you've been gaslighting me. That ends now. If Rick entered your web willingly while knowing the risks, I say he should be held responsible too. Because you know who is not at fault? Me. I am not going to sacrifice anything: not my integrity, not my future, not my sanity for two people who have treated me as badly as you and Rick have treated me. Don't call me again." She ended the call and dropped her phone to the floor.

Leaning over her knees, she started to sob. Her family was gone. Richard's thieving had completely stolen that from her. There would be no reconciliation with Rick, not after all the horrible things he'd said to her, all while knowing that his father was to blame. All while using her as a shield for his own criminal behaviour.

"Oh, Babble." Kat leaned down and hugged her. "I'm so sorry."

Barb kept to her room for the next two days, only leaving it for meals and coffee. Her heart ached for her family, but at the same time she knew that she hadn't seen her family for who they truly were. She spent hours wrapping and rewrapping the gifts she'd bought for Kyle and Rick.

Depending on her mood, she would end up with dark and dreary packages or over-the-top presents better suited to young children. Usually, they ended up somewhere in between, but every time the gifts were wrapped, she would cry.

Rick kept calling and because she wasn't answering her phone, he would leave messages. She wasn't ready to listen to them yet. Not until she was ready to decide what to do.

Because as much as she wanted to tell the police where they could find Richard, she struggled with being even a tiny bit responsible for her son going to prison.

She had done nothing wrong and yet she was in this predicament. She hated Richard for doing this to her but she could not hate her son. Anger, fury yes, she felt that towards Rick, but she couldn't hate him. But not hating him didn't mean she thought he should be free from consequences. He'd known what Richard was doing and not only had he not stopped his father, he'd joined in. And then he'd pretended to be a victim all while blaming her.

She crept out into the living room. It was late morning and there was no sign of Kat. Barb sighed.

Her friend had been supportive and kind and caring, but Barb didn't want any more pitying looks.

The coffee was still warm, so she poured herself a cup and sat in the living room, staring at her phone. She really couldn't put it off anymore. She had to make a decision, which meant she had to listen to the five messages Rick had left her.

The first three were pretty much what she expected. He asked her to call him so they could *sort this out,* but by the third call she could hear the stress and frustration in his voice. On the fourth message, he finally apologized for not telling her that he knew where his father was. But there was no apology for how he'd treated her: for the months of silence and the angry phone call.

She played the fifth message and shook her head. He was furious. And to be honest, in the past, having her son furious with her would have sent her scurrying to do whatever she had to in order to placate him.

But not now. Let him be furious. She was furious too: with him. But it helped her make her decision. Rick's anger told her that he wasn't sorry for what he'd done, he was only sorry that she knew. And that she had the power to decide who else might learn the truth about his actions.

The doorbell rang. Thinking that Kat was expecting a delivery, she opened it.

Rick stood on the porch.

"Mom. We have to talk."

"Do we?" She regretted sending him her address when she moved here. How like him to use it to come and demand her time and attention for this.

"Come on," Rick said. "You're not going to leave me out here in the cold, are you?"

She stepped away from the door so he could enter the house and walked back to the living room. She sat down without offering him anything to drink, something that the old Barb would have been horrified at. But this wasn't a social call.

"I'm sorry I didn't tell you about Dad," Rick said as he sat on the sofa across from her.

"So you said," she replied. "In one of your messages."

"He told me he talked to you. That you, uh, know where he is."

"I do," Barb replied.

"He said that you're not going to tell the cops."

"Did he? Why *wouldn't* I tell the police? It would shift suspicion off me so that I can put the hell of the last half year behind me and get on with my life."

"But he said . . . ," Rick paused. "He told you what would happen to me."

"He did," Barb agreed. "But you didn't care about what was happening to me. In fact, I seem to recall you blaming me. All this time you knew. And *worse*, you were part of it."

The front door opened. "Barb, whose car is in the driveway?" Kat called.

"It belongs to my son Rick," Barb replied. "We're in the living room."

"Does she know?" Rick asked. He looked worried.

"Yes. You think I can hide something like this from my best friend and roommate?" Barb asked. "I am not your father."

Kat was still wearing her coat when she joined them. She stood behind the chair Barb was in but didn't say anything.

"How many people know?" Rick definitely sounded worried.

"Me, Kat, and Kat's grown daughter," Barb replied.

"Crap." Rick dragged a hand across his eyes. "It's too late, isn't it? I'm too late."

"It's never too late to do the right thing," Barb said. "That's advice that I will be following, so if you're talking about me making sure the police know where to find your father, yes, it's too late."

"What about me? You're all right sending me to prison?"

"*Stop it!*" Barb said. She was so mad she was shaking. Kat put a hand on her shoulder and Barb took a deep breath. "You don't get to blame me for this. *You're* the one who knew what your father was doing. *You're* the one who made the choice to get involved in it. None of this is on me! Get out."

"You're really going to send me to prison? What kind of mother are you?"

"The kind who is incredibly disappointed in you," Barb said. "The kind who taught you that there are consequences. It's not my fault you chose to believe your father when he told you that there wouldn't be."

"I'll see you to the door," Kat said.

"Screw you, Mom," Rick said as he stood up. "Hope you're happy."

"Of course, I'm not happy," she said. She closed her eyes as he walked past her.

She heard murmurs at the door and then it closed.

"I gave him my number," Kat said, "and told him to call me if he decides he wants to be the one to talk to the police. They might cut him some slack if he confesses."

"Thank you. He wouldn't have listened to me."

"I know. And I'm sorry."

"Me too." She tried to smile. "I guess I can return that damned tie clip. Rick won't take a gift from me now."

"Offering to let *him* tell the police is a gift," Kat said. "Don't you forget it."

CHAPTER 13

WITH ONE WEEK to go before Christmas, Barb decided to throw herself into holiday preparations. It would her very first Christmas without her family: Rick had stormed out of her life two days ago and she assumed he would turn Kyle against her too.

So rather than just mope, she decided to get into the holiday spirit *and* mope.

When she was done, she was pretty sure she'd spent every last nickel she'd earned gift-wrapping, but she wasn't going to let that stop her from making the absolute most of what she *did* have instead of lamenting what she didn't.

It was hard though, and she told Kat to ignore her if she suddenly got teary-eyed or had to leave the room for a moment.

But the house and small tree were finally decorated and she was even making mulled wine. The tie and cuff links would eventually be returned, but her gift to Kyle went under the tree. She was going to drop it off at his condo. She could wait until Boxing Day or even the new year. It wasn't like he would need a bicycle pump in winter. Besides, she had no idea if he was even staying in the city. The past few years he'd been going on ski trips for the holidays, and Barb thought it likely Kyle would head out again this year.

"Who wants mulled wine?" Barb asked.

"Me," Mitch replied.

"And me," Kat echoed. "Do you need some help?"

"Come and grab a mug." Barb ladled wine into three mugs and slid two of them across the island. Kat took them and set one down beside her daughter before sitting down with the other.

Barb brought hers into the living room and settled on the couch, cradling the drink in her hands.

"The house looks great," Mitch said. "Mom might be an artist but she's never spent much time decorating."

"When you were a kid, I had to use all of my creative energy to earn enough to feed and clothe us," Kat replied. "And in the past few years, it didn't seem worth it." She turned to Barb. "But it is worth it. This is lovely, thank you."

"You're welcome," Barb said. "There's a lot about this Christmas that makes me sad, but spending it with the two of you is the happy part of the holiday. I wanted the house to reflect that." Between the mulled wine and the real tree, the house smelled as good as it looked.

"There's been no word from Rick," Kat said. "Stupid man."

"Then Mitch, I need you to contact Crime Stoppers," Barb said. "I'll wrap something in case Richard has gone somewhere else."

"Maybe that's what Rick is waiting for," Mitch said. "If Richard has left Costa Rica, then giving the police his address there won't hurt anyone and Rick will be seen as cooperating."

"He should still have called me or Kat," Barb said. She didn't have any hope that Rick would do the right thing, not when he'd been doing the wrong thing with his father for years.

The doorbell rang.

"I'm not expecting anyone," Kat said as she got up to answer it.

"Barb," Kat called from the door. "It's for you."

Barb raised her brows at Mitch. She wasn't expecting anyone. Her eyes lit on Kyle's present. Unless her younger son had come for a visit?

But no. A man and woman stood on the stoop. One was

holding out a badge.

"Barbara Baker?" the woman asked.

"Yes," Barb replied.

"I'm Detective Sergeant Singh and this is Detective Malone from the Hamilton Police Service. We need to speak with you."

Barb's heart raced. "What's happened? Are my sons all right?" Would Rick harm himself rather than face consequences for what he'd done?

"Your son Rick is fine," Detective Sergeant Singh said. "But he has given Toronto Police information regarding your husband's whereabouts. Information he says came from you."

"I'm sorry, Kat," Barb said to her friend. "We'll stay in the front hall for our chat."

"All right," Kat said to the detectives. "I'll be in the living room if I'm needed."

Kat gave her a wide-eyed look as she went past Barb.

Barb backed up to let the two detectives into the small hallway.

"Did my son mention that he already knew where his father was and that he'd spoken to him?" Barb leaned her back against the wall and did her best to remain calm despite her fury. Rick was trying to pin the blame on her. She would tell the cops the truth, even though they wouldn't believe some of what she said.

"My notes don't mention that," Detective Sergeant Singh said. "How do you know that?"

"Because I found out where Richard was and texted that information to my son," Barb said. "A few hours later my husband called me."

"I see," Singh replied. "And when was this?"

"A week ago," she said.

"Why didn't you call the police then?"

"Because my husband told me that if I did, I would expose Rick's involvement in his embezzlement scheme. I needed some time to process that news."

"Your son said that you would blame him," Malone said.

"Did he?" She shook her head. How had she not realized what kind of man Rick was? For the same reason she never recognized that her husband was a thief: she hadn't wanted to. "I'm sad but not surprised. I was hoping he would do the right thing, but I guess I gave him enough time to figure out another wrong thing."

"What do you mean?" Singh asked.

"My friend advised Rick to go to the police and tell them where his father was; that the police might be lenient if he helped them catch his father." Now she was glad she'd kept all of Rick's voicemail messages. She'd listened to them a few times, and there was definitely enough there that made him sound suspicious.

"The friend who answered the door?" Singh asked.

Barb nodded and the Detective Sergeant nodded at her partner. "Detective Malone will question her. You stay here with me."

Barb heard voices from the living room and a few minutes later Malone returned.

"The story checks out," Malone said. "And we've been asked to come into the living room. There's another witness."

"Then by all means, let's talk to everyone." Singh gestured to Barb to lead the way.

"I made coffee," Mitch said. "Anyone want one?"

The two detectives declined but Barb nodded. She didn't need the caffeine but it would give her something to do with her hands.

Once Mitch had set a coffee in front of her, she relaxed.

"I am going to tell you how I found out where my husband is," Barb said. "You won't believe me, but it's the truth." She squared her shoulders. "I wrapped presents for him and my sons, and the gift tags I wrote with their names changed to where Richard was and what I think are the bank names and account numbers where the money is. Because my son Rick was no longer taking my calls, I texted him the town and country. A few hours later, my husband called me. That's how I know that Rick knew how to contact his father."

"Back up," Singh said. "What you wrote on the gift tags *changed*?"

"Yes," she said. "I'll get them. They're in my room." She hurried down the hall and grabbed the presents for Rick and Richard, glad she hadn't found time to return them, along with the tag for Kyle's gift since it was under the tree.

She was about to head back to the living room but paused. She'd rewrap Richard's gift; maybe if they saw it with their own eyes, they'd believe her. She opened her supply of gift-wrap and after a moment made a few selections. Then she carried everything out to the living room.

She put the wrapping supplies on the floor next to the couch and handed the wrapped presents and Kyle's gift tag to Detective Sergeant Singh. "These are the cards. It's my handwriting but I didn't write what's on them."

"Can anyone confirm that?" Malone asked.

"Not for these," Kat spoke up. "But I witnessed the same thing three times a few weeks ago."

"Really?" Singh didn't sound like she believed them. "You're in danger of making me question the truth of your statement about your conversation with your son, Rick Baker."

"We're not lying," Kat said. "Even though it seems unbelievable."

"I'll show you," Barb said. "I was going to do this again anyway since I doubt my son has told you where his father is right now."

"You think he waited until Richard Baker had left Costa Rica before contacting the police?" Singh asked. "And you're telling me that you'll be able to tell where he went with a gift tag."

"Yes," Barb said when she really meant she hoped to hell she could. She carefully unwrapped the tie she'd picked out for Richard and cut new paper to fit the box. A few minutes later, the gift was beautifully wrapped. She took a deep breath before picking up a gift tag. She passed it to Singh who studied it, handed if off to Malone, who then gave it back to her.

Barb set the tag down on the coffee table and with her pen wrote *To Richard*. She then slid the tag across the table to Singh, who covered it with her hand.

"What the . . ." Singh's words trailed off. "I saw you write *To Richard*. I'm going to need you to use my pen."

"All right," Barb said, trying to hide her relief. Richard must have fled Costa Rica. "And for the record, I have not seen what the tag says." Barb put a second gift tag on the table, took the pen

Singh held out to her, and again wrote *To Richard*.

Singh grabbed the tag almost before Barb finished writing. She set the pen on the table, picked up her coffee, and took a sip. It was no longer hot but she took another sip anyway.

"How did you do that?" Singh asked.

"I have no idea," Barb said. "I've never done anything like it before. As Kat said, it started a few weeks ago."

"The incident at the Canadian Makers Christmas Show," Malone said. "You were accused of stealing something because you knew where it could be found. That was because of something like this?"

"It was." Now Barb was grateful for that whole terrible ordeal. "I wrapped a gift, and what I wrote on the gift tag changed to the name of a pawn shop I didn't even know existed. The police were called and I was accused of stealing."

"Yes," Malone said. "I questioned the officer involved. He said that surveillance showed that the daughter of the woman who accused you pawned the item. But he had no idea how you knew where the missing item was."

"You've seen me do it," Barb said. "Do you believe me?"

"I don't know what I believe," Singh said. "I will hand these tags to Toronto Police and let them determine whether any of this"—she waved the tags—"is factual." She stood up. "Don't leave town. Malone."

Malone stood as well. He tucked his notebook in a pocket and pulled out a business card. "Call me if you find out anything else," he said. Singh was already in the hallway. "About anything," Malone said softly.

"Sure." Barb took the card on the coffee table while Kat followed the detectives to the front door. She heard the door shut and then the lock turned.

"Well, that was a waste of time," Kat said. "I don't think they believed what they saw with their own eyes."

"Malone did," Barb replied. She waved the business card at her friend. "He asked me to call him if I find out anything else. Then he added 'about anything' when his partner was out of earshot."

"I'm not sure that means he believes you," Mitch said.

"No, but I think it means he is keeping an open mind," Barb replied. "Which I can't say about Detective Sergeant Singh."

"Yeah," Kat agreed. "She's already decided that whatever you did is some sort of trick."

"I know." Barb sighed. "She'll be back when they track Richard down to whatever new place he's fled to."

"Which is where?" Mitch asked.

Barb grabbed a third gift tag. "Let's find out." She wrote *To Richard* once more, then picked up the card. "Varadero, Cuba," she read out loud. "He always did like the beach."

"That's a tourist spot," Mitch said. "I have friends who went to a resort there a few years ago."

"Then he's probably staying in a resort," Kat said. "Enjoying the high life. Let's hope the police can track him down."

"That should be pretty easy," Barb said. "He would have had to use his passport to get to Cuba." Without knowing where to look, finding her husband would be a monumental task. Without knowing where to look. Even though she knew the police would be back to question her, she grinned. Not only had she turned the tables on her son, she'd told the police where to find her husband. Consequences indeed.

CHAPTER 14

BARB WAS HALF afraid that she wouldn't be able to write Kyle's name on the gift tag. It had been two days since the police detectives had come to see her, and she'd heard nothing. Not from the police, not from Rick, and not from Richard.

The police had told her not to leave town, but she didn't think they meant she couldn't drive into Toronto to leave a gift for her son.

She'd planned on doing it after Christmas but she needed something to do right now. It would also give her a chance to stop by the St. Lawrence Market and buy a few of her usual holiday treats and try to pretend her whole life and family hadn't collapsed since last Christmas.

She covered the holiday wrapping paper with plain brown craft paper and pulled out a gift tag and a marker. She hesitated for a moment, worried she couldn't write his name on the tag. But her strange talent remained dormant when she wrote down her son's name and condo unit number. Did that mean there was nothing else related to Kyle to be found? Or just nothing to worry about? She hadn't known about either the lost brooch or the pawned vase. It was frustrating not having any clear-cut rules to this talent of hers.

Barb said goodbye to Kat, put the double-wrapped gift in the back seat of her car, and drove to the Queen Elizabeth Way.

Traffic was steady but not nearly the start and stop crush of rush hour. She tuned in a radio station that was playing Christmas music and sang along as she drove.

The closer she got to the centre of the city, the more crowded the roads were. She took the Jarvis Street off-ramp and then turned south to Queens Quay. At Kyle's condo building, she pulled into a visitor parking spot and took the gift inside.

A harried concierge asked her to put the gift on the counter with half a dozen others and slid a clipboard across to her before he was pulled into a conversation with two other people.

Barb filled out the form: a description of the package, who it was for, the date and time, and then she signed it. The concierge nodded, initialled beside her signature, and took back the clipboard.

That was it. Her gift for Kyle was delivered and she hadn't even had a chance to ask if her son was still in town. Outside the building, she sighed. She was tempted to drive to Rick's house, but she wasn't ready for a confrontation with either him or his wife. Not today, not when she was doing her very best to be in a Christmas frame of mind.

And then guilt flooded her: what if Rick's wife, Margot, like her, had no idea that her husband was a thief? The last thing she wanted was for anyone else to deal with the crap she'd had to deal with.

But other than tell her daughter-in-law what Rick had done—which would undoubtedly lead to a confrontation—Barb didn't see a way to help.

She'd support her after the fact, she promised herself. If Margot was blindsided the way she had been, she'd need someone in her corner.

Barb had a favourite side street where she always parked when she shopped at the St. Lawrence Market. It never failed to yield a spot and this time was no different.

The market was busy but she was able to get everything on her list. The final item was lunch: peameal bacon on a bun. It was the St. Lawrence Market signature sandwich as evidenced by the signed pictures of celebrities and celebrity chefs who had visited the bakery take out counter.

After eating, Barb strolled along Front Street. She always enjoyed the understated elegance of decorations on the row of old warehouses and the way sparkling lights outlined the roofline of the Flatiron Building.

Snow began to fall and she turned towards her car. It was time to go home.

Home. It no longer meant the house she'd expected to live out her old age in or the people who were her family. Instead, it meant a small bungalow in the Hamilton neighbourhood she'd escaped from so many decades ago. And a friend who had become her family.

Barb said goodbye to Christmas in Toronto and drove out of the city.

After her trip to Toronto, Barb felt on edge, like she was waiting for the other shoe to drop.

Two days before Christmas, it did.

"We have some news, Mrs. Baker."

The two detectives, Singh and Malone, were at the front door.

"Come in." She stepped back to allow the two enough room to enter the house. "Kat Henderson, the owner of the house, isn't here right now."

"We don't need another statement from her," Singh replied. "And we'll be brief. The information you gave us checked out. Richard Elliot Baker and a companion were living in a house in Montezuma, Costa Rica until a few days ago. The bank accounts you gave us were recently closed and the money transferred out, but they belonged to Elliot Baker. And again, per your information, when the two left Costa Rica, they flew to Cuba."

"But you didn't get any of the money back," Barb said. "Nor have you caught Richard." Perhaps his companion—what's-her-face—would leave Richard and he'd be all alone and on the run. The less fun he had, the better she liked it.

"We have not," Singh said. She shifted her feet and Barb couldn't help raising her eyebrows.

"He's left Cuba and you want me to find out where he is now," she said. "So, you believe me. You believe the gift tags."

"We believe you somehow can find your husband," Singh said. "So yes, if you can, we would like you to tell us where he is." She held up a hand. "However, we are going to ask you to do that down at the station. We'll supply the gift-wrap."

"All right," she said. "I can come right now."

Singh frowned but Malone smirked.

"Thank you," Singh said. "We'll meet you at Central Station in an hour. Ask for me at the desk."

"Can't wait," Barb said.

Detective Malone lifted his chin to her on his way out the door. Was that because he thought she would show his partner that she was the real deal? That he believed she really did have a supernatural ability that allowed her to find Richard? Because Detective Sergeant Singh *did not* believe her. Singh had seemed almost disappointed that she'd so quickly agreed to come down to the station. Perhaps she'd expected Barb to decline and would have taken that as proof that she was a fake.

Barb grinned. She wasn't a fake and she didn't care if the police knew it. Her grin slipped. But her ability to find things didn't always work: what if it didn't work in front of the police? Then they wouldn't believe her and she wouldn't be any worse off than she was.

She left a note for Kat on the kitchen island saying that she should be home later that afternoon. Then Barb picked up the tie she'd wrapped for Richard, got in her car, and drove downtown.

She just wanted this over, and if proving to the police that she could find Richard with gift-wrapping would do it, then she was all for it.

She found a spot in the parking lot across from the blocky, brick building that housed the police station. When she asked for Detective Sergeant Singh at the desk, they asked her to wait to one side.

The inside of the building was as uninspiring as the outside: too much brown brick and too little personality.

She was studying the smooth brick floors when a door opened.
"Ms. Baker, this way."
She looked up the see Detective Malone holding a door open.
"Will I have an audience?" she asked as she headed past him.
"Of course," he replied. "And you'll be filmed as well. Is that a problem?"
"Nope. If someone here can explain to me how I do what I do, I'd be grateful."
"Sometimes there is no explanation."
"You believe me." It wasn't a question and he didn't answer. Instead, he gestured to an open door up ahead. When she walked into the room, Barb was greeted by Detective Sergeant Singh. The room was bare except for some very gaudy wrapping supplies on a table and three basic wooden chairs. There was a mirror along the back wall, and she was tempted to wave: if TV was anything like real life, then one or more people were watching from behind the mirror.

She put the wrapped tie on the table.

"I brought something to wrap," she said. "But you can check it to make sure there aren't any tricks."

She sat down in one of the chairs. She actually felt better knowing that at least one cop believed she really could do this.

"Can I unwrap this?" Singh asked.

"Yes. I haven't touched it since I wrapped it in front of you a few days ago. So please, make sure it's just a tie."

While Singh dealt with the tie, Malone pointed to a camera up in one corner. "That camera will record everything from that angle. We are also having a mobile camera delivered. Ah, there it is."

A man carried in a camera and set it up on a tripod. "Where do you want it pointed?"

Malone looked at Barb. "We ask that you keep your hands on the table at all times."

"Sure," Barb replied. She put her hands flat on the table top.

"Then point the camera at her hands," Malone told the camera operator.

"Wand this, Malone," Singh said. She held the tie in one hand

and the other held out the same sort of wand device Barb had seen in airports. Malone took the device, switched it on, and passed it over the length of the tie.

"Clear," he said. He then took the tie and handed the device to Singh, who did the exact same thing.

"All right," Singh said. "Wrap up that tie and tell us where Richard Elliot Baker is now."

Barb took the tie from Malone and laid it out on the table. It would be better in the box but she didn't think they would let her use that. Instead, she started folding the gift-wrap so that it at least gave her some structure. She placed the tie in the paper and continued wrapping it. She tied a ribbon around it to secure the package before pushing the wrapped tie into the middle of the table. Then she pulled a gift tag towards her. With the pen supplied, she wrote *To Richard* and then dropped the pen and lifted her hands away from the tag.

"Did you catch that?" Malone asked.

He was looking at the camera operator, who nodded. "I'll play it back."

Barb looked down at the gift tag that now said *Podgorica, Montenegro*. Richard was in Europe now. She wanted to laugh: he hated the parts of Europe where most people didn't speak English. She very much thought that included Podgorica, Montenegro.

Singh and Malone crowded around the camera. No one commented, but Barb could tell from the expressions on the faces of Detective Sergeant Singh and the camera operator that what they saw surprised them.

Malone looked past the camera and met her eyes and almost imperceptibly lifted his eyebrows.

"Shall I write out another gift tag?" Barb asked.

"Yes," Singh said.

Barb's hands were still on the table and she dragged a second gift tag in front of her. "Do you want to bring the camera closer?"

"Do it," Singh said, and the camera operator slid the tripod over until the camera was pointing directly over Barb's left shoulder.

She picked up the pen and wrote *To Richard* on the tag, dropped the pen, and lifted her hands. Again, the tag said *Podgorica, Montenegro.*

Singh's phone rang.

"You seeing this?" she asked as she stepped to the mirrored wall. "I don't know." There was a pause. "I see."

Singh turned back to Barb. "I have no idea how you're doing this but Montenegro does not extradite criminals back to Canada."

"But you still don't believe me," Barb said. "That I have some weird supernatural talent."

"All this proves to me is that you have done your homework," Singh replied. "And that you have a sleight of hand writing talent. But you can go home. Again, don't leave town."

Singh frowned and left the room. The camera operator folded up the tripod and followed her, closing the door behind him.

"So that's it?" Barb asked Detective Malone. "I did everything I was asked to do and I'm still a suspect?"

"It's Detective Sergeant Singh's case," he said. "But can I ask you a favour? We're also looking for your husband's, uh, companion."

This time Barb did laugh. "Are you telling me Richard had her do something illegal? You don't need to answer that. Yes, I will help you find her. I need something to wrap."

"How about this?" Malone held out a piece of paper. "It's a warrant that we want to serve her with."

"Perfect." Somehow this made the trip down here worth it. She selected the ugliest wrapping paper from the bundle and made an envelope and got ready to stuff the warrant inside.

"Do you already know her name?" Malone asked.

"Oh, I know it," Barb replied. "I just won't use it." She slid the warrant into the gift-wrap envelope, taped the edge shut, and grabbed a gift tag. She wrote *what's-her-face* on the tag, dropped the pen, and raised her hands off the table.

Malone leaned over the table. "Veradero, Cuba," he read. "Looks like he left her behind."

"Or she decided that life on the run wasn't as glamourous as she thought it would be," Barb replied. "Check for new waitress hires at the resorts. Richard has a weak spot for servers. Can I go now?"

"Yes," Malone replied. "And thank you."

"Sure. Next time you need me to put on a show, you can just call. I've done nothing wrong so I'm not going anywhere."

She stood up and when Malone opened the door, she walked through it.

She waited until she was in her car before bursting into laughter. Barb knew that if Detective Sergeant Singh was watching she would look suspicious, but she couldn't help it. Not only was she positive Richard *hated* the European country he was in, but he was alone! Even what's-her-face had left him. She hoped their breakup had been bitter and accusatory and full of drama because every one of those things would make Richard angry.

Barb buckled her seat belt. And she was the one behind it all! She was the reason her husband's well-thought-out plans weren't working. She and her unexplainable gift tag magic.

"Karma, Richard!" she yelled as she drove away. "Karma!"

CHAPTER 15

"Montenegro," Kat said. "What's there?"

"Apparently a country that doesn't extradite criminals to Canada," Barb said. She'd stopped on her way home and texted Kat that she was bringing dinner. Now they were eating take-out Swiss Chalet Festive Special chicken dinners. Barb was definitely feeling festive.

"Richard did his homework," Kat said. "I guess I'm not surprised. But you think the police still consider you a suspect."

"Toronto Police, probably," Barb said. She speared a slice of chicken and dipped it into the sauce before eating it. "Hamilton Police?" She shrugged. "Detective Sergeant Singh doesn't believe her own eyes. Detective Malone believed me even before I did their little test."

"I guess that's good," Kat replied.

"I didn't tell you the best part," Barb said. "After Singh left, Malone asked me to try to find what's-her-face." Barb grinned. "She stayed in Cuba. Richard is all alone in Montenegro. For Christmas."

"Is that good?"

"It's bad for Richard," Barb said. "He hates being alone almost as much as he hates being in a country where they don't all speak English. And the holidays were always a time for him to act like a big shot. I know he'll just find some other impressionable young thing wherever he is, but the one he planned to run away with is done with him." She ate the last few fries and pushed her plate away. "And so am I. From now on I'm going to concentrate on me and let my family deal with whatever problems they've created." She'd thought about this on her way home from the police station. After her intense glee at Richard's predicament, she worried that she could be consumed with revenge and spend her time trying to make his life more difficult. That would hurt her more than it would hurt him.

Besides, if she truly wanted to be done with Richard and the control he had over her life, she had to leave his fate up to the police.

"I can help with that," Kat said. "But I'm sure the police will keep you informed. And it would be perfectly normal to feel satisfaction that Richard is dealing with the consequences of his actions."

"I'd also feel satisfaction if at least some of the money can be recovered," Barb said. "He hurt a lot of people." She still felt terrible that she'd been—however unwittingly—a party to Richard's stealing. All those dinner parties and charity events she'd hosted where Richard held court and attracted more *investors*. Although some were wealthy, she knew many could not afford to lose what Richard had stolen from them.

"None of it was your fault," Kat reminded her.

"I know," Barb agreed. Her previous upbeat mood had evaporated. "But I still feel guilty." She stood up. "I'll clear up. Why don't you find us something to watch on TV?"

For the first time after everything that had happened in the past few weeks—no, make that the past six months—Barb slept soundly and woke up refreshed and truly ready to start her new life.

Richard was a problem she'd done her best to resolve, and the rest was up to the police, and maybe fate. She was content that he wasn't living the relaxed life of luxury he'd planned—that had been unconscionable to her—and grateful that she'd had a hand in him losing that.

It was Christmas Eve, and yes, it would be a sad holiday without her family, but as she'd discovered, her family wasn't what she'd thought anyway.

She'd make new traditions with Kat and Mitch, and in the New Year, she would build a business using this gift of hers.

She was the first one up. While she waited for the coffee to brew, she checked out the lost pet website. She had four messages from people looking for help finding their pets.

Barb set her coffee on the dining table and then grabbed a few supplies from her room. Her coffee grew cold but in minutes she had four wrapped gifts with name tags with clues.

After online searches the first three seemed pretty straightforward: the name of a park, an intersection, and a person. Hoping that she wasn't giving anyone bad news the day before Christmas, she replied to those emails.

The last gift tag was a puzzle because the name on the tag hadn't changed to a clue. She wrote out two more gift tags but the name she wrote stayed put. Wondering if the gift wasn't good enough for Buster, she wrapped different flavoured dog treats. The tag still said Buster.

Barb sat back and frowned. Maybe the dog wasn't really lost?

"What's wrong?" Kat asked as she entered the kitchen.

"I'm looking for a lost dog," Barb replied. "But the gift tag isn't changing."

"Ooh, coffee. Want some more?"

"Sure." Barb stared at the gift tag while Kat refilled her mug.

"Did you wrap something the dog likes?" Kat asked as she sat down across from her.

"I've wrapped two different items," Barb said. "And I've written four gift tags. I have to assume the dog is not missing." If she couldn't be sure of her talent, then her business was in trouble before she even got started.

"Maybe they found it already," Kat said.

"They must have. I'll ask the person who wrote to me."

She pulled up her phone and replied.

The doorbell rang.

"I'll get it," Barb said. She headed to the front door, wondering if Mitch had decided to come over early. She still had tons to do before she put the Christmas Eve tourtière in the oven.

She opened the door and froze.

"Hi, Mom." Kyle stood on the stoop. "Sorry I didn't warn you I was coming. I got your present and I wanted to say thank you in person."

"Kyle," Barb managed to stammer. "I wasn't expecting you. Oh, that sounded terrible. I'm really happy to see you. Come in." She stepped back and her son followed her into the house.

"The coffee is still hot if you'd like a cup," Barb offered. Kyle didn't seem angry, like Rick had when he'd visited. "Here, let me take your coat."

"Thanks," Kyle said. "I would love a coffee."

Barb hung her son's coat in the front hall closet. "This way." She headed to the kitchen. "Kat, I'd like you to meet my youngest son, Kyle. Kyle, this is my oldest friend in the world, Kat Henderson."

"It's nice to finally meet you," Kat said. "I think Barb offered you coffee. I'll get you a cup and then I have some things I need to do in the workshop."

"Please sit down," Barb said, gesturing to the living room. "Kat is a jewelry maker. She turned her garage into a workshop."

"Cool." Kyle sat on the chair and Barb sat on the couch across from him.

"I wasn't sure what you wanted in your coffee," Kat said, putting a tray down on the coffee table. It held two mugs of coffee as well as a pitcher with milk and a bowl of sugar.

"Black is good but thanks," Kyle said.

"Let me know if you need anything," Kat said. She sent a pointed look to Barb before leaving the room.

"She seems nice," Kyle said.

"She is," Barb replied. "We reconnected a few years ago. Your father broke up our friendship when he and I got married."

"That jerk," Kyle said.

"Yes." Barb sipped her coffee. She wasn't exactly sure why Kyle was here but hearing him describe his father that way gave her hope. "I'm glad you liked the bicycle pump," she said. "I always had a hard time knowing what to get you."

"It's great. I have something for you but it's in the car. I thought we should talk first. Rick called me."

"To quote you, *that jerk*," Barb said. She was happy that Kyle had come to visit, but if he was going to pull the same crap on her that Rick had, she'd tell him to leave.

"Yep," Kyle agreed. "But what he told me means that I owe you an apology."

"What?" This was not what she'd expected. Kyle agreeing that his brother was a jerk *and* an apology. "An apology for what?"

"I thought you were in on it too," Kyle said. "I thought that you, Dad, and then Rick were all criminals. But I was wrong. I'm sorry I lumped you in with them, and I'm sorry for all the grief that caused you."

Barb took in a shuddery breath. Finally, someone in her family was acknowledging the horrible ordeal she'd been through. "It wasn't your fault," she said. "But when did you know they were criminals?"

"I've suspected Dad for a few years," Kyle said. "I even invested money with him to try to figure out what he was doing. It didn't work but I got a good look at what an incredible liar he is. Then last year Rick came right out and told me what was really going on. He thought I'd want to be part of the *family business*, as he termed it." He sighed. "And what happened to you *is* partly my fault. I'm the one who got the whole investigation rolling. I reported them to the authorities. And I told them that you were part of it."

"You what?" Barb was stunned. "But you've hardly visited the family for years. Oh, I see. Ever since you suspected your father."

"Yeah. After Dad blew me off when I expressed concerns about my investment." He shrugged. "In my line of business, I can't afford to ruin my reputation by hanging around criminals. Even if there's no proof of wrongdoing and even if they're my direct family."

"But you never said anything." Barb was still confused. "And you work in a technology startup. Do they care that much about your reputation?"

"I lied about that," Kyle said. "I don't work for a startup. I work for the federal government in a role that I'm not allowed to disclose to you."

"Holy cow." Barb had watched enough Netflix to know what that meant. "You're a spy."

"I work with computers," Kyle said. "And my boss knows I'm here. And please know that coming here was my idea, but because you're still under investigation—even though that's in part because of me—I had to get permission to visit you." He paused. "I am more sorry about this than I can say. My boss wants to know how you knew where Dad was."

Barb sat back. Her son was maybe not quite a spy but he probably worked with spies. He'd had to get permission to see her. Because they all thought that she was a criminal. "Your boss wouldn't have let you visit me unless you promised to ask me that." No wonder he hadn't spent a lot of time with the family over the past few years: his work wouldn't allow it.

"Yes."

"Everyone wants to know," she replied with a shrug. "Including me. I did a demonstration for the Hamilton Police yesterday. There's no harm in doing another one. Who or what would you like me to find?"

"You don't mind?" Kyle asked. "I thought you'd be angry."

"Like I said, I'd like to know how I do it too. I mean, I know what I need to do to find lost things, pets, and people, but I don't know *why* it works."

"Okay," Kyle said. "There's a very specific coffee mug at my office that keeps disappearing. Can you tell me where it is?"

"I'll do my best." She looked around the room. "Pick something here that you would like me to give you. I think it has to be something you would actually like but I'm pretty new at this."

"Some of that sugar," Kyle said. "I've been on a low sugar diet for a few weeks and the cravings haven't gone away yet."

"All right." Barb went to the kitchen and came back with a small zipper bag. She spooned some sugar into it and then picked through the wrapping supplies she had brought out for the lost pets. When the small bag was wrapped, she picked up a gift tag.

"I have to ask if you trust me to wrap this," Barb said. Kyle nodded. "This is the interesting part. Watch closely." She wrote *To Kyle* on the tag and then sat back.

"What? That is not what I saw you write."

Barb leaned forward. The tag said *Final Boss*. "Who or what is Final Boss?"

"It's the nickname for my boss's boss. I need to make a call."

"Sure. I'll go check on Kat." Barb left her son to call his maybe not quite-a-spy boss and knocked on the door to Kat's workshop.

"Is he gone?" Kat asked.

"He's making a call," Barb said, closing the door behind her. "I'll explain that part later. Kyle's the one who called the cops on Richard. He said Rick invited him to participate in the Ponzi scheme, and that he thought his whole family—including me—were criminals. Apparently, he suspected Richard was doing something illegal but couldn't prove it, so he was trying to stay away from all of us."

"Wow," Kat said. "Wow."

"I know." Barb paced the length of the workshop. She wasn't sure what she was allowed to tell her friend about her son's work, but Kyle hadn't told her not to say anything. She'd wait to ask him, just the same.

"Mom?" The door to the house opened and Kyle poked his head into the workshop. "Sorry about that. The coffee mug was right where you said it would be. I've been given permission to explain things to your friend. And make you an offer."

While Kat made a fresh pot of coffee, Barb and Kyle sat in the living room. Nervous, she picked up her phone. There was a response to her email about the dog Buster. It turned out he hadn't been lost after all: Buster showed up right on time for his dinner.

Barb smiled.

"Good news?" Kyle asked.

"Just a dog that wasn't lost after all," Barb said.

"Is that the one where the gift tag didn't change?" Kat asked as she brought a tray of coffee into the living room.

"That's the one," Barb said. She picked up the wrapped gift and lifted the tag. "Buster."

"You're finding lost dogs?" Kyle asked. "That's such a nice thing to do."

"The first thing I ever found was a young girl's lost cat," Barb replied. "And I'm not being all that nice. I'm trying to figure out how I can use this thing I can do to make a living."

"Ohh, right." Kyle looked horrified. "You're not part of the Ponzi scheme, so you don't have a secret stash of cash. Oh Mom, I am so sorry. I have some money set aside that I can give you."

"Thanks, Kyle. I'm not saying I will never take you up on your offer but I'm good for now. Besides, I need to figure out how to support myself long-term." Taking money from her son would only delay the inevitable.

"At least I can help with that," Kyle said. "I'm authorized to offer you paid work. I have no idea what the long-term needs would be but initially there would be quite a lot to do." He paused. "There are a lot of missing Richard Bakers out there."

"What if I can't find them all?" Her son hadn't denied that he was a spy but this sounded more like law enforcement. If Kyle's job entailed searching for criminals, then it was no wonder he'd been distancing himself from his family.

"If you can find any of them, then it will be better than we've been doing," Kyle said. "These are all cases where any trail, digital or otherwise, has gone cold. Even finding out that they are dead will allow us to close the file."

"Then yes," Barb said. "As long as you and your boss understand that I am not sure how I do what I do and that I can't guarantee results."

"No problem. I'll text you the contact information for the person who will be handling your assignments. You probably won't hear from them until after the holidays."

"That sounds good." Barb could hardly believe that not only did her son believe she had nothing to do with Richard's embezzling, but he was also embracing her strange, new ability.

"All right," Kyle said standing up. "I have to get back to the office. Um . . ."

"I'm cooking tomorrow," Barb said quickly. "You're welcome to join us. It's just me and Kat and Kat's daughter, Mitch. And you and whoever you'd like to bring. Unless you're off on your annual ski trip."

"I can't tomorrow," Kyle said. "I'm actually working. It's how I've spent the past two Christmases." He shrugged. "I lied about being away for the holidays."

"How about New Year's?" Kat asked.

"Yes, please come," Barb said. Kyle had deliberately spent Christmas alone rather than be with his criminal family. Yet another thing for her to be angry at Richard for. "I'll cook a big meal. You don't have to commit right away; just call or text me when you know."

"I already know I'm free on New Year's Day," Kyle said. "And I'd love to come."

"Perfect," Barb replied. "I'll make a ham. Let's plan for midday."

"It's a date," Kyle said. He pulled out his phone and glanced at it. "I really do need to get going."

"I'll get your coat." Barb led the way to the front hall and pulled Kyle's coat from the closet.

"I'm so glad you dropped by," she said.

"Me too." Kyle zipped up his jacket. "I'm sorry about everything and that I can't be with you on Christmas. But it looks like you have a really great friend to spend it with. So that's good."

"It is good," Barb agreed. "I'll see you on New Year's Day."

Kyle nodded and reached in to hug her, and she squeezed him tight before letting go and stepping back.

"Drive safe," she said.

"See you, Mom."

And then he was out the door. She stood watching through the window as he walked to his car. When he was gone, she headed back to the living room.

"I did not expect that to happen," Kat said.

"Me neither." Barb sat down and grinned. "But it's good. It's really good."

"It's great," Kat said. "He doesn't think you're a thief and he's coming for New Year's Day dinner."

"It is great." She was still sad about Rick but at least one son was willing to see her. It was a much better holiday than she'd expected just a few hours ago. And to top it all off, Kyle's work was willing to pay her to use her weird talent.

CHAPTER 16

STILL BUOYED BY Kyle's visit, Barb hummed Christmas carols while she mulled some wine and heated up the tourtière Kat had bought at a local shop. Mitch arrived late in the afternoon. Barb poured them all mugs of mulled wine while Kat filled her daughter in on Kyle's visit.

"He works for the government?" Mitch asked. "After telling you for years he worked for a tech start-up?"

"It all sounds very secretive," Barb said. She put the tray of mugs on the coffee table. "And when I asked him, he didn't actually deny being a spy." She picked up a mug and cradled it in her hands. "What he did say was that he works with computers."

"And he seems to hunt down people who have stolen money and have fled the country," Kat added. "I think he must work for Canada Revenue."

"He mentioned that 'there are a lot of missing Richard Bakers'," Barb said. She'd been thinking about her conversation with Kyle all afternoon. "But that doesn't mean he doesn't search for violent criminals too. Does the government have more than one department working on their cold cases?"

"The government is pretty departmentalized," Mitch said. "But the investigative computer skills required for that type of work are pretty specialized. A guy from Common Cause ended up working for the government and he was never clear which department. His expertise is on how individuals are being targeted for surveillance through technology, not searching for people who have fallen off the grid, but there aren't that many people in the country with that level of expertise, let alone ones who work for the government. The consensus for the Common Cause guy was that he works for *all* departments. It's possible Kyle is the same."

"He stopped seeing his family because he thought we were all a bunch of criminals," Barb said. "I assume that was because it could compromise him somehow."

"Or maybe he just thought it wrong to hang out with thieves," Kat replied. "Sorry Barb, I know that Rick's involvement hurts."

"I'm more angry than hurt," Barb replied. "How dare he call the police and point the finger at me when he's the one in the wrong. And that's after months of telling me I was at fault for Richard's misdeeds."

"Classic gaslighting," Mitch said. "Trying to get you to believe something that you know is wrong. Have you heard any more from the police?"

"No and I don't want to." Barb sipped her wine. "Let's change the subject. It's my first Christmas as a single woman, and I don't want to spend it talking about the men who have treated me badly."

"That sounds like a very good idea," Kat said.

"I sometimes have them," Barb agreed. "More wine?"

"Another good idea," Mitch said.

Barb woke early on Christmas Day. She'd wrapped the small items she'd bought for Kat and Mitch last night, and now she snuck out to place them under the tree before Kat got up.

She plugged the tree lights in, placed the gifts under it, and sat down to enjoy how it looked. There wasn't much under the tree; certainly not the mountains of expensive items that the Baker tree usually sported. For years she and Richard had fought about the extravagant gift-giving for adults, including their sons, Rick's wife, neighbours, and some of Richard's business associates.

She always wanted to cut back and give gifts to family only: for her Christmas was more about spending time together than getting and giving presents.

Richard always won that argument though: what if people showed up with gifts and *he* had nothing for them? How could he ever look them in the eye again? Except all of the gift purchasing was up to her, and if the gift was liked, he took credit, but if it wasn't suitable, she was blamed. She hadn't fully appreciated it at the time, but the stress of the holidays had been intense.

All because of Richard's need to impress people, which in hindsight was all about him finding more investors he could steal from.

Kat and Mitch's tradition of giving small, inexpensive gifts and spending a quiet day with each other was so much more relaxed.

Coffee in hand, Barb checked her phone. There was a text from Kyle wishing her a Merry Christmas along with the name of the person she would be dealing with for the paid work. Soula Stavros would contact her after the holidays. There was no mention of a department name, and Barb wondered if Soula would tell her something fake. As long as she could claim the income for her taxes, she really didn't care.

Kat joined her an hour later and after that Barb had to get the turkey into the oven.

Early afternoon saw Mitch arrive, and then they had a traditional Christmas dinner followed by a walk on the windswept beach along the shores of Lake Ontario.

Mitch went home after that, and Barb and Kat returned to the house and drank eggnog while they cleaned up in the kitchen.

All in all, it was a lovely, restful day, and Barb only felt a few pangs of sadness. She didn't really miss her old life—her old Christmas—but she did miss her family. Not Richard of course, or Kyle, who she would see in a week. Rick was the one she mourned: the son she worried would be lost to her forever. But she went to bed that night pleased with herself; she'd made it through the most difficult holiday. Not unscathed, but mentally and physically in one piece.

That was an accomplishment after the year she'd had.

And Kyle was coming for dinner on New Year's Day. Things could be worse.

CHAPTER 17

KYLE ARRIVED MIDMORNING. Barb beamed as she hugged him. He'd been in touch a few times during the past week: two texts and a phone call yesterday confirming the time and asking if he could bring anything.

"I forgot to give you this when I was here before Christmas," he said, handing her a small wrapped gift.

"Thank you," Barb said. She took the gift and led the way into the living room, setting the present down on the coffee table.

"Kyle, you met Kat Henderson last week, and this is Mitch, Kat's daughter. Dinner will be in an hour and I have to do a few things in the kitchen."

The open plan main floor meant that Barb could still see the others in the living room and could follow their conversation. Mostly small talk about the season, the weather, and of course, the traffic Kyle had endured on the drive from Toronto.

The crackling on the ham was browning nicely, so all Barb had to do was toss the already washed potatoes with oil and get them in the oven to roast. Halfway through she'd take them out, smash them, and add some herbs.

She filled a pot with water and set it on low for the squash.

"Can I get anyone a drink?" she asked across the kitchen island.

"You sit," Kat replied, hurrying over. "I'll get drinks. We still have some eggnog."

"That's fine with me," Barb replied. "No rum though."

"Are you going to open your present?" Mitch asked when Barb sat down on the couch beside Kyle.

"It's not nearly as impressive as the bike pump," Kyle said. He handed it to her.

She carefully unwrapped it, revealing a small box. When she opened the box, her jaw dropped. "My grandmother's ring. This was sold as part of the estate." She looked at her son. This was her last, true family heirloom, but she'd parted with it in the hopes it would help repay even a little bit of what Richard had stolen. "How did you get it?"

"I bought it," he replied. "It belonged to my great-grandmother. I didn't think it would mean as much to someone else. When you gave me the bike pump, I realized that the Christmas presents that meant the most to me were all from you. And that the ones that were about prestige or money or status were picked by Dad. So, I tried to return the favour and give you something meaningful."

"It's the best present ever." She brushed away a tear. "I thought this was gone for good. Thank you." She laughed. "It doesn't even fit me, so I've never worn it." She'd offered it to Rick when he was ready to propose to Margot, but he'd told her she was being ridiculous. Instead, he'd bought his fiancée a huge solitaire diamond.

"Maybe you should get it fitted," Kat said. "Now that you aren't wearing your wedding and engagement rings."

Barb held out her left hand. She'd taken her wedding band and engagement ring off to wrap the wedding band and find her husband. She hadn't bothered to put either back on, and although she didn't miss wearing them, her hand always looked a little bare.

"I don't really miss them," Barb said. "Which is weird after wearing them for so many years. I need to sell those rings." The wedding band was pretty basic but the engagement ring should be worth something. Her wedding photos had been proof that she'd owned the ring before Richard's Ponzi scheme started, which was the only reason why the police let her keep it.

"January isn't a bad time of year for it," Kat said. "A lot of people get engaged or married on Valentine's Day."

"I am still legally married," Barb said. "Which I guess is something I should take care of in the new year."

"And change your name back to Fabel," Kat said.

"Yes." Barb raised her glass of eggnog. "To the New Year. Let's hope it's better for all of us than the old year was." She didn't see how this year could be any worse than the past one, but she didn't want to tempt fate.

"This was great, Mom," Kyle said. "I have always said that you make the best smashed potatoes. It seems like a simple thing but I've never even come close."

"The trick is to buy the right type of potatoes," Barb said. "And smash them halfway through."

"Another delicious meal, Barb," Mitch said. "Kyle, I'm sure I don't have to tell you that your mom is a great cook." Mitch stood up. "My mom is better at the clean up so we'll do that."

"Let's give them some space," Barb said to Kyle. "Want to take a walk?"

"Sure, some fresh air would be nice."

"We'll just be in the neighbourhood," Barb called as they headed to the door.

Once they were bundled up in coats and boots and scarves, the two headed outside. The sidewalk hadn't been cleared of snow, so they walked on the road in the ruts left by tires. The day had been grey and cloudy, but now the light was shifting as the sun tried to make an appearance.

"Kat and Mitch seem nice," Kyle said. "I'm really glad you have them. I feel terrible that I'm the reason your life has been so difficult this past year."

"I'm glad I have them too," Barb said. "And they are nice. And you weren't the one working an elaborate Ponzi scheme for decades, so I don't see how any of this is your fault. If you hadn't reported your father, this would have come out eventually." She'd been thinking about this ever since Kyle had told her that he was the one who reported it. "I honestly believe that your father's scheming was finally catching up with him. I think that's why he already had a place to run to and money stashed overseas."

"Maybe," Kyle said. "But you might not have been blamed."

"People are right to blame me," she said. "I didn't do anything wrong but I certainly didn't question where the money came from. Even I can't believe I was so stupid."

"Not stupid," Kyle replied. "Trusting. Dad was an actual professional at getting people to trust him: that's why he was able to part so many people from their money. The fact that he got you to trust him shouldn't be a surprise."

"It still is to me," Barb replied. "I ignored all the warning signs. He didn't want me to work nor did he want me involved in anything financial, including dealing with the house bills. I had no idea he'd remortgaged the house. I thought it was fully paid for. Jeez, we even had a celebration dinner when he told me we were mortgage free. Why didn't I ask to see the paperwork?"

"You think he wouldn't have just created something to show you?" Kyle asked. "Scammers go to great lengths to make sure they aren't questioned."

"That's what he is, isn't it? A scammer, a thief, an embezzler. I feel horrible that he was stealing from everyone we knew. And that I helped him by being the consummate hostess." She shook her head. "All those people must hate me."

"You're a victim too," Kyle said.

"I guess," Barb said. "But I feel more like an accomplice. Unwitting and unwilling, but Richard Baker wouldn't have been able to steal quite so much for quite so long without me."

"He would have found someone else."

Barb's laugh was bitter. "He *always* had someone else and I let that go too." They reached a cul-de-sac. The escarpment loomed above them, and the sun broke out, making the snow on the trees glisten.

"Yet another thing that I shouldn't have ignored or let Richard talk his way out of." She sighed and paused to look up at the escarpment. "It definitely would have been better for me to get out of my marriage sooner, but even a few years later would have been even more devastating. At least now I have enough time to rebuild my life." She shrugged and met Kyle's eyes. "So, you contacting the police was actually a good thing for me. Come on, let's head back. I could use a coffee."

"Same here," Kyle said.

Barb was explaining her business idea to Kyle when they turned onto Kat's street.

"You've got to be kidding. What's he doing here?" Kyle said.

"Who?" Barb stared up the street. "Oh." It was Rick. She recognized the coat he was wearing from the last time he'd visited her, when he'd had the nerve to be angry that she wasn't willing to cover up his crimes.

"I'll deal with him," Kyle said. "You stay here." He headed down the street towards his brother.

"To heck with that," Barb said under her breath. Letting men—her husband in particular—handle things was one of the reasons she was in the predicament she was in. She was not going to do that again.

She heard her sons' raised voices before she reached them.

"Maybe you can continue this inside?" she asked. As much as she didn't want to inflict this on Kat and Mitch, she preferred that option to annoying the neighbours.

"Rick was just leaving," Kyle said. "Weren't you?"

"Mother, just what the hell have you done?" Rick said to her. "The cops are looking into my finances."

"I told them the truth," Barb replied. "When they had me come down to the police station to interview me because of what you told them. After Kat gave you a way to help yourself, you doubled down on blaming me. You *know* I had nothing to do with the Ponzi scheme."

"How could you?" Rick said in a low voice. "You've ruined me."

"And there's the Rick I've always known," Kyle said. "Never taking responsibility for your own terrible decisions: it's always someone else's fault. If you want to blame someone, then blame me. I'm the one who blew the whistle on Dad last year. *After* you offered to let me in on the *family business*." Kyle shrugged. "When I found out that Mom had nothing to do with any of it, I might have suggested to someone, somewhere that they should take a closer look at you." Kyle met Barb's eyes. "Sorry, I didn't tell you. I didn't think my jerk brother would show up here."

"You're the jerk," Rick said. "What kind of brother are you?"

"The kind that won't cover up your crimes," Kyle said. "The kind that expects you to be responsible for your actions. And if you won't do that willingly, then you need to be forced to."

"Jesus," Rick swore. "I should have left the country when Dad told me to. I hate both of you." He glared at them, then stomped back towards his car.

"I'd be able to find you anyway," Barb called after him. "Just like I found your father." Rick sent her an angry look before he got into his car and backed out of the driveway.

As he sped off, Barb's anger turned to sadness.

"How Rick turned out is not your fault," Kyle said. "Trust me, he's always been an entitled jerk."

"How did I not know?"

"He hid it from you," Kyle said. "He's a good liar. There's a reason Dad allowed him in on the scam."

"I guess." She looked up to see a worried Kat in the doorway. "Come on. I need to apologize to Kat for bringing all of this chaos to her house, especially during the holidays."

CHAPTER 18

"For the last time, I don't blame you," Kat said.

Kyle had left an hour ago, and Barb had asked Kat how she could make up for ruining her New Year's Day.

"I kinda appreciated it in a weird way," Mitch said. "Not your pain and suffering, of course, but I've heard about terrible family fights during the holidays, and Mom and I don't do that, so to actually see one was interesting."

"Mitch," Kat said. "That's not helping."

"It is, actually," Barb replied. "This is probably not the only family fight that happened today." She sighed. "Although I'm pretty sure the others weren't about calling the police on family members involved in illegal activities."

"You don't know that," Kat said. She and Mitch turned to each other.

"The Sinclairs," they said in unison.

"They lived down the street when Grandma was still alive," Mitch said. "They used to have loud parties that often ended up in fist fights."

"The police were here weekly during the summer," Kat said. "Then one Labour Day, a dozen cop cars descended on their house. It tuns out the family was growing pot up on the escarpment. One drunken brother got mad and called the cops on his brother, not thinking it through well enough to understand that he would be charged too."

"I was in grade eight," Mitch said. "We kids all knew where the pot was but we'd been warned about messing with it. The Sinclairs moved out a few months later."

"And—" Whatever Kat was going to say was interrupted by the sounds of three phones sounding an alert.

"Amber Alert," Mitch said, looking at her phone. "A five-year-old boy."

"Cue horrible people calling 9-1-1 to complain," Kat said. "No doubt this missing child is interfering with them watching their football game."

An Amber Alert. Barb sat back in her chair. They always made her sad; children taken from their homes would be worried and confused and scared. She hated that.

But this time she might be able to help. This time she might be able to find the child.

"I need to get some gift-wrap," she said out loud. "And a gift tag."

"Oh wow," Mitch said. "You need to try."

"Yes," Barb agreed. "I need to try."

"Is there anything else we can do to help?" Mitch asked.

Barb shook her head in frustration. This was her second attempt at finding the child—a boy named Noah Taylor—and the gift tag had not changed. What was she doing wrong? "Maybe I need a better gift?" The picture of Noah showed him in a shirt with a dinosaur on the front. They didn't have an actual toy dinosaur, so Kat had printed off some pictures of some.

"Maybe it's like the dog that wasn't lost," Kat said.

"Oh." Barb sat up. "Maybe the child doesn't feel lost. Maybe I should wrap a gift for the mother. She's the one who reported him missing." It was hard not knowing the rules about how her talent worked.

"That's worth a try," Kat replied. "The missing pets were all reported missing by people."

"Yep," Barb agreed. "That one dog was safe at home but the

other pets *were* lost. Or at least not with their owners." The first cat she hadn't been able to find had been with the ex. "But I was able to find Richard by wrapping a gift for him and he would not think of himself as lost."

Kat shrugged. "That might have been because *you* were looking for him: he was lost *to you*."

"Maybe. I'll wrap a gift for the mother. I think I can wrap the same thing." She made a new envelope out of gift-wrap, took the printed pages out of the other one, and slid them into the new one. "Oh, I don't know the mother's name."

"Let me search," Mitch said, picking up her phone. After a few minutes, she sighed. "I can't find it."

"All right. Meanwhile I'll see if *To Noah's Mom* works." Barb wrote that on a gift tag, set it on the coffee table, and sat back.

"Nope," Mitch said. "Still says *To Noah's Mom*."

Barb picked another gift tag and wrote *To Noah Taylor's Mom* on it. She stared at it but nothing changed.

"Either I need her actual name or the gift itself isn't right," Barb said.

"We need to find out her name," Kat replied. "You wrapped an empty box for that woman from the retirement home and that was enough to find her lost jewelry."

"You're right," Barb said. "But how do we find out the mother's name?" She stood up. "I know. I'll ask the police."

"Are you sure?" Kat asked, but Barb was already halfway down the hall.

She went past her bed to the side table. Was it here? Yes. She grabbed the card and headed back to the living room.

"They won't believe you," Kat said. "If you tell them why you want her name."

"This one will." Barb held the card up. "Detective Mike Malone already believes me. He told me to call him *about anything*. This is something."

Barb picked up her phone and punched in the numbers from the card. And heard Malone's recorded message. It was late at night on New Year's Day, of course he wasn't in the office. The beep sounded. "Detective Malone, this is Barbara Baker. You told me to call you about anything. So, here it goes. I'm trying to find Noah Taylor, but since nothing has worked so far, I'd like to know his mother's name. In case that helps me. If I don't hear from you, I will assume I misunderstood your comment to me." She left her phone number and hung up.

"That's it," she said. Her phone said it was after ten. "I'm too wired to go to sleep, so I think I'll try to watch TV or something."

"I'm with you, Barb," Kat said. "I don't think I can sleep. I'm going to make some herbal tea. Who wants some?"

Barb raised her hand.

"No thanks, Mom," Mitch said. "I'm going to head home." She kissed her mother on the cheek. "Keep me posted. And Barb, it's a good plan even if it doesn't work out."

"Thanks." Barb stared at her phone. The Amber Alert message was still there although there hadn't been any more alarms.

She heard the front door open and close, and a few minutes later, Kat sat down across from her.

"The kettle is on," Kat said. "And Mitch is right. Even if you can't help find this child, it's a really good thing to try."

"I guess."

Barb couldn't have explained the movie. It was halfway through, and she'd been thinking about the Amber Alert instead of following what was on the TV. Her phone rang and she snapped out of her fog. She picked up her phone: the number was blocked and it was after midnight. It had to be Detective Malone. Or maybe Richard was calling to yell at her again.

"Hello?"

"Ms. Baker," a man said. "I apologize for returning your call so late. I hope I didn't wake you."

"Detective Malone?" Barb sat up, and across from her, Kat turned off the TV. "I couldn't sleep. Does this mean you're willing to help me?"

"You're the one offering to help," Malone said. "Do you really think you can find the boy?"

"I haven't been able to so far," Barb replied. "We think—that is, my friend and I think it might because the child does not think he's lost. That's why I'm asking for the mother's name."

"This didn't go out in the alert," Malone said. "But the search team believes the boy's babysitter has him."

"So, he's safe?" Barb was relieved. Even if she didn't find little Noah, he was with someone who wouldn't harm him.

"An Amber Alert wouldn't get approved if law enforcement thought he was safe," Malone said. "I don't know those details but I was able to get the name of the mother. Do you want it?"

"Yes."

"Hailey Delacruz," Malone said. "Sorry, I don't have anything more than that."

"I'll see what I can do," Barb said. "If you can wait, I'll put you on speaker."

"Sure."

Barb put her phone on the coffee table.

She grabbed a fresh gift tag and pulled the wrapped gift towards her. "Here we go," she said to herself and wrote *To Hailey Delacruz* on the gift tag. She turned it over and held her breath before flipping it right side up.

"I have something," she said. "The number sixteen and the words *Safe Travels* but safe and travels are capitalized."

"There's a motel named Safe Travels just outside of Niagara Falls," Kat said. Barb looked up to see her friend staring at her phone. "Maybe that means he's in room sixteen."

"Thanks," Malone said. "I'll do a little more digging and then let the search team know. I'll keep you posted."

"Will you have to tell them it came from me?" Barb asked. Now that she'd come up with a clue, she was worried that helping would add more chaos and disruptions to her life.

Malone chuckled. "I wouldn't dare. Detective Sergeant Singh was livid when we got the notice to drop our investigation into you, hand over the videos we took, and forget that we ever met you. I'll say the info came from an anonymous tip. But, Ms. Baker? I appreciate the help. I don't know who or what you're involved in that can make your file disappear, but my offer is still open. You can call me about anything. Thanks again." The call ended and Barb sat staring at her phone.

"Kyle may not be a spy," Barb said to Kat, "but it sounds like he works with some. Who else would be able to make a police file and videos of me disappear?"

"Babble Fabel," Kat said. "Who would have thought you would end up with such an interesting family."

"*Interesting*," Barb repeated. "Sure. A husband who is a world class embezzler, one son who is following in his father's footsteps, and another who works for some sort of spy agency. Sounds like a dream."

"You're forgetting someone," Kat said. "The wife and mother who has a supernatural ability to find lost people, pets, and things. Like I said, interesting."

CHAPTER 19

"BARB," KAT CALLED from outside Barb's bedroom door. "Are you awake?"

"I am now." Barb pushed the covers off and swung her legs to the floor. She'd finally gotten to sleep around four and she didn't feel rested. "Come on in."

"They found the boy," Kat said as she entered the room. "At a motel just outside of Niagara Falls. You did it!"

"Really? He's safe? That's great."

"And it's a good thing you did find him," Kat said. "It turns out that the babysitter was in some sort of online relationship with a suspected pedophile from the U.S. He'd somehow convinced her to bring the boy to him but then he got stuck and couldn't get across the border."

"Oh wow." Barb shivered. "That poor child. At least he's safe."

"Thanks to you," Kat said. "Come on, I'll make you a ham and cheese omelette. And I promise, I can make a good one."

"I'll be right there." Barb picked up her phone. Sure enough, there was a text from Detective Malone telling her that what she'd told him was correct and had led to the safe recovery of the boy.

There was a second text from an unfamiliar number introducing herself as Soula Stavros and asking for Barb to suggest a time for them to meet in person. It took Barb a moment to remember that this was the person Kyle said would be in touch. She grinned. It looked like she was soon going to be earning some money.

Barb threw on her robe and headed out to the kitchen. She had a life to start living.

THE END

About the Author

JANE GLATT LOVES that along with creating original worlds, writing fantasy allows her to indulge her curiosity about an eclectic group of subjects. So far, she's researched synaesthesia, medieval guilds, tidal rivers, cities atop bridges, pirates and privateers, plants used for healing, and the history of spying. For that last one she blames a visit to the International Spy Museum (yes, it's a real place), in Washington, D.C.

For news on Jane's future releases, visit her website http://janeglatt.com/index.html and sign up for her newsletter.

Milton Keynes UK
Ingram Content Group UK Ltd.
UKHW041922171124
2895UKWH00001B/1